He had a decided talent for trouble

As a banker, Richard Trenton knew his position was tricky. And he didn't relish the assignment his superiors had foisted on him: to find the missing will of one of their most prestigious clients, who'd recently died.

But Richard had an uncanny ability for unearthing facts—something the police regarded as interference...

...and grudgingly came to appreciate when he exposed a bizarre crime.

Anne Burton

WORSE THAN A CRIME

A RAVEN HOUSE MYSTERY FROM

W🌐RLDWIDE

TORONTO · NEW YORK · LOS ANGELES · LONDON

It is worse than a crime, it is a blunder.
　　　　　　　　　　—de la Meurthe

Raven House edition published November 1982

Second printing

ISBN 0-373-63046-8

1

"I'VE NOTHING WHATEVER to do with the Trustee Department," said Richard Trenton flatly. "So if you want to transfer me there you'd better bloody well get on with it and let me know where I stand."

Edward Jarvis, one of the more energetic of the joint general managers of the Northumberland and Wessex Bank, eyed his subordinate with a sort of humorous benevolence. Confident of getting his own way, he could afford to overlook his subordinate's remarks. Jarvis was a small man, probably about sixty, and Richard had for some time suspected him of having a sense of humor, though working conditions in the Advance Department of a large bank didn't make it exactly easy to tell. Now, however, he was sure of it. The man had a sense of humor, and rather an unkind one at that. It didn't occur to Richard, indignant as he was, that there was anything at all funny about his own reaction. He was normally a mild-tempered man, not given to strong language (which in any case Maggie, his wife, frowned on in front of the children), and the only thing that was obvious to him at that moment was that Jarvis had been looking for a rise and had got one.

In the Advance Department there were two sections that looked after the Greater London area, and Richard Trenton was the controller of one of these, B section. That morning he hadn't expected Jarvis to be in the bank at all, because he knew there was no general managers' meeting. The summons to meet his superior had disturbed the schedule he had set for himself that day, which was an added annoyance, and now to be asked—

"I don't think you can have quite understood what it is I want you to do," said Jarvis patiently. "I'll start again from the beginning."

"I know the Hampstead branch is in my section," said Richard, ignoring this, "but there isn't even any borrowing involved."

"There wouldn't be with a man as wealthy as Jock Thorold," said Jarvis.

"Well, then, if it's a matter about his estate, surely the Trustee Department—"

"You haven't been listening," said Jarvis. This time his tone was a little sharper. "The Trustee Department doesn't come into it; our client died intestate."

"Well, there are laws about that. And I have been listening," Richard added, not altogether able to keep a mutinous tone out of his voice. "Only it all seems such a rigmarole."

"Then I must try to be a little more lucid," said Jarvis. "What do you know of Jock Thorold?"

"Nothing at all until you mentioned him just now. As you said yourself, the question of a loan has never arisen, not since I joined the department anyway. And I'm pretty sure he wasn't a customer of any of the branches I was at before I came here."

"I should be surprised, however, to learn that you haven't heard of Tam O'Shanter Clothing. They do enough advertising in all conscience."

"Yes, of course I have—cheap suits off the peg," said Richard a little scornfully. "And not so cheap nowadays," he added. He was a dark man, perpetually at war with his hair, which inclined to wave, and he was one of those people who find it quite impossible to look untidy, no matter what chores they are engaged in.

"You needn't sneer about it," Jarvis told him. "I'm afraid you haven't got a proper approach to money, Richard."

"There's a lot involved, is there?"

"There certainly is. Thorold died recently—I hope you gathered that much from my discourse—at the age of seventy-eight. His father was a tailor, and that's where he learned his trade, but when he was in his early twenties he decided the money was in mass production. For obvious reasons, availability of cloth and so on, he fixed on Leeds for his head-quarters, though you'll gather from the name of the firm that he was rather determinedly Scottish, and in the course of time he had outlets all over the country. He came south about twenty-five years ago; I suppose he felt by that time that everything was running smoothly without his constant supervision, though he still made fairly frequent trips to Leeds. Anyway, he bought himself a place in Hampstead Heath—almost a palace, Bob Blake says it is." (Blake was the manager of the Hampstead branch of the bank.) "Bob has no idea of the exact extent of his holdings, though he has managed numerous small transactions for him over the years. Including the one concerning the boy."

"A lad called Malcolm Stonor," said Richard reflectively—perhaps with the intention of showing the older man that he hadn't been completely inattentive.

"That's right; he's twenty now. Jock took him to live with him five years ago when Malcolm's mother died. He sent him to school and then paid for his articles with a firm of solicitors in the City. He arranged for an allowance for him and told Bob he meant to see Stonor well established in life. They had some conversation about that, Bob will tell you himself. And then Jock Thorold died without having made any provision for his protégé.''

"What about the family? If there's so much money, surely they'll carry out his wishes.''

"That's where you come in," said Jarvis, not without a certain sadistic satisfaction. "Though none of them admit he has any claim at all against the estate.''

"If he wasn't a relative, why did Thorold more or less adopt him?''

"Bob has a theory about that. But there was no adoption; that's the whole trouble.''

"What does Bob Blake think?''

"Just that the old boy wanted a son very badly. What he got was three daughters.''

"Is his wife still alive?''

"No, she died ten years or so ago.''

"Tell me about the daughters, then.''

"The eldest is Eleanor, then there's Geraldine, and then Alexandra.''

"And they all have it in for the wretched boy?''

"It would seem so.''

"Three spinsters?'' Richard asked.

"No, they're all married. That's part of the trouble, I expect: they all have families.''

"The families, I suppose, will be somewhere about Malcolm Stonor's age?''

"Some older, some younger.'' Jarvis spread his hands, obviously a little vague himself on the subject.

"The husbands, then?''

"Eleanor is married to a man called Philip Lawson, who happens to be a solicitor. I understand from Bob that it has been agreed that he shall ask for letters of administration.''

"That seems the obvious thing, certainly.''

"Yes, I think so. Geraldine is married to Maxwell Fielding, who is an architect, and Alexandra to

Wilfred Bennett, a builder and contractor. I understand the two men have a good many business con-
nections. So what I want you to do, Richard, is to go
and see this Philip Lawson—''

''Yes, I did take that much in. But I don't understand; it's no concern of the bank's what happens
to the estate.''

''Jock Thorold has been a customer of ours for
years, both in the north and here. Bob Blake feels
very strongly that his wishes should be honored in
this matter of the young man. At the same time—I
want you to understand this very clearly, Richard—
nothing must be done to offend any of the beneficiaries.''

''They're all clients of ours, too, I suppose,'' said
Richard in a grumbling tone.

''Exactly. And when I say the beneficiaries, I
mean not only the daughters but their husbands,
too.''

''Then why not just leave it?''

''I thought better of you, Richard.'' Jarvis was
quite obviously enjoying the situation that he had
created. ''I seem to remember having heard you
preach on the theme that banking should be a matter of principle, of ethics, rather than an adherence
to the strict letter of the law.''

''Yes, I do think so, but—''

''Then there's nothing more to be said. Bob Blake
agrees with you, and in this instance I'm willing to
accommodate him.''

''Why can't *he* go and see this Philip Lawson?''

''I happen to think that you're the man for the
job.''

''But really, sir—''

''Not another word, Richard. You've conducted
two delicate investigations in the past without offending anybody and without compromising the
bank in any way.''

"But this isn't an investigation!"

"No, it's something much simpler, but the delicacy of touch is still needed. I think you should see Bob Blake, and then perhaps one of the partners in Fulford and Hughes, the firm where Stonor is articled. Their office is practically next door to you."

"Yes, I know, in Bread Court. I've met Jake Fulford and got on well with him, but I don't see how talking to him can help me."

"He's another solicitor, isn't he? He may have a trick or two up his sleeve," said Jarvis blandly. "Now, I'm sure I can rely on you, Richard, to carry out this matter to everyone's satisfaction. After all, when it's pointed out to Lawson that his father-in-law had expressed a definite desire to see Malcolm Stonor settled, I'm sure that will make a difference."

"I still don't see why Bob Blake couldn't do it."

"He very properly referred the matter to us," said Jarvis, as if that concluded the matter. "I'm merely communicating our decision to you." He consulted his watch and added inconsequently, "Let's see, it's Thursday. I've arranged for Blake to meet you here for lunch at twelve-thirty, and for John Kent to cover anything urgent that arises in your section for the rest of the day and tomorrow. If you require any more time—"

I see what it is, said Richard rebelliously, but he had the good sense to say it to himself and not aloud. You don't want the Trustee Department on the job at all; you want a ruddy diplomat.

II

Bob Blake was a bulky man, about ten years Richard's senior, who looked as though he crammed himself only with difficulty into conventional garb. Before the hour of their meeting arrived, Richard had already communicated his discontent to John Kent, who was by way of being his closest friend in the department, and made his excuses for not joining him as usual for lunch. "If you ask me," said Kent sapiently, when he had considered the matter a little, "Jarvis has something up his sleeve beyond what he told you."

"That may well be," said Richard. "All I know is it will be my fault if any of these precious clients of ours are upset by my activities."

"Did he spell that out for you in so many words?"

"He certainly did. Though nobody needed to; I know Jarvis's ways well enough," said Richard, and made his way down to the executive dining room where Blake had already settled himself at a corner table.

"It's good of you to take this on," he said with genuine feeling when Richard was seated opposite him. "I don't mind telling you the whole business has me stymied."

Remembering Jarvis's own frequently expressed feelings, Richard did not say again, "I don't know what it's got to do with us." Instead, "If it had to be done, why couldn't you do it yourself?" he inquired disagreeably.

"Now, don't tell me you grudge me your help." Bob Blake was hurt by this ungraciousness, and Richard was immediately contrite.

"I didn't say that. But I don't think I'm particularly noted for my tact."

"All you Advance Department chaps know how to say no," said Blake, who had come to his present position from another branch. "If you can cope with that, you can cope with anything."

There was a certain amount of truth in that remark, though Richard wasn't altogether convinced. "Do you know all these people?" he asked.

"Yes, I do, or most of them, and that's partly

why—someone from head office. It sounds much more important, much more likely to impress them.''

"If they did but know," said Richard bitterly. "Talk about being a dogsbody. However, I've two questions to ask you, Bob. The first is, why does Malcolm Stonor's fate matter so much to you? And the other is, what can you tell me about Jock Thorold's family?''

"It's not so much Malcolm Stonor," said Blake. "He seems a nice enough young fellow, but I haven't had any dealings with him until the past couple of years. But the old boy—Jock Thorold— had something about him. I don't know quite how to put it, something very likable, and he was quite clear about his intentions.''

"Haven't you at least pointed that out to Mr. Lawson?''

"I didn't have a chance to; he was telling me what the family meant to do.''

"I see. Then perhaps, Bob, you can tell me exactly what Mr. Thorold said to you.''

"He took the boy in about five years ago. Did Jarvis tell you that?''

"It's one of the few things he did tell me. That, and something about Mr. Thorold's background. I gather he was a self-made man.''

"He certainly was, and proud of it. I think that's probably what I found so engaging. Anyway, I heard that Stonor had gone to live with him in a roundabout way, not from Jock himself. I also heard that he was sending the boy to school. It wasn't until two years ago that he came to me—the old man, I mean—to make arrangements for a regular allowance for Malcolm, and told me he was being articled with a firm in the City.''

"Fulford and Hughes. I know them," said Richard.

"Jock said he'd been making investigations, and they were a good, well-rounded firm. Malcolm would get experience on the family side of the business and also in criminal work, if his tastes lay that way."

"Yes, that's Jake Fulford's speciality," Richard agreed. "What I can't understand," he added inconsequently, "is why Jarvis is concerning himself on the boy's behalf."

Bob Blake looked at him curiously. "Didn't he tell you?" he asked.

"Oh, he put it all on a highly moral plane," said Richard in a discontented tone. "I didn't believe it for a moment."

"I expect he thought that would appeal to you," said Blake, to Richard's annoyance, who didn't think himself any better than the next man. "However, if you'll let me get on with my story, I think everything will become plain to you."

"All right, then, get on with it."

"At that time—when he arranged about the articles—Jock said he meant to see Malcolm through the five years of his training and then look round for a firm in which he could purchase him a junior partnership. After that he mentioned the subject to me from time to time, at first on the same lines, but later he told me quite categorically that he'd decided to leave Malcolm the business in Leeds."

"I gather that's pretty valuable—"

"It certainly is!"

"—but doesn't it form the bulk of the estate?"

"Not from what he told me. He said he had always been careful with his money, invested it wisely, and that it would be fair enough to his daughters: they'd each get an amount just about equivalent to the factory's value. They're not interested in the business, of course, and neither are any of their husbands. It's been running pretty well

with the management Jock put in. I think his trips
north were more because he wanted to go than because he had to. But he said he didn't want it sold;
you never knew, the purchasers might get someone
incompetent in, and it wouldn't be fair to his work-
people. Their welfare seemed to be something that
meant a great deal to him. Malcolm's inheriting
would be conditional on his keeping it going on the
present lines, and keeping a general eye on things,
even though his interests lay in a different direction. So that's how Jock wanted it to be.''

"Yes, I understand that. Now, I gather he died intestate.''

"I did venture to take the matter up with him
once,'' said Blake. "He was one of those people I
felt instinctively would imagine it unlucky to make
a will. I don't know whether I was right about that
or not, but certainly at that time he hadn't done so,
just said there was plenty of time, he wasn't going
to die just yet.''

"But—''

"Oh, I pointed out Malcolm's position to him, of
course, asked him straight out why he had never
adopted the boy. All he would say to that was, 'No
need, no need.' At that time I didn't feel I could
take it any further, but the next time he mentioned
the factory to me I asked him if his intentions were
still the same. He said they certainly were, he
wasn't one to change his mind—that was true
enough. So I felt it my duty to bring up the question
of a will yet again.''

"And what did he say to that?''

"Oh, he grumbled a good bit—did I think he was
in his dotage, that sort of thing. But eventually he
promised to do something about it.''

"How long ago was this?''

"About six months ago. Yes, I remember now, it
was just before Christmas.''

"Did he ever tell you if he'd followed your advice?"

"No, and I didn't bring up the subject again. I knew the kind of answer I'd get: his word was as good as his bond, wasn't it?"

"Who is his solicitor?"

"I think his son-in-law, Philip Lawson, dealt with everything like that for him."

"If the family disapproves, as it seems they must do, of Malcolm getting anything at all, perhaps he felt a little awkward about going to Lawson in that particular matter."

"Oh, Jock never felt awkward about anything in his life," said Blake positively. "All the same, he might have gone to somebody else. But it's a week since he died now, and there were obituaries in most of the papers as well as the regular announcement. I think if that had been the case someone would have come forward."

"Yes, so do I. What did he die of?"

"He fell downstairs and broke a hip. Things went wrong, as they so often do with old people in similar circumstances—pneumonia, I suppose. I was sorry to hear about it, I can tell you that; he was one of my customers I was really fond of."

"And an excellent account," said Richard a little dryly.

"Yes, that of course."

"Though I suppose the factory's account was in the north of England?"

"Yes, it was."

"I am beginning to understand Jarvis's concern. If Malcolm Stonor can prove his claim in some way...it doesn't seem very likely, but I suppose the bank has to cover all its options."

"I knew you'd understand, Richard. You do realize it needs careful handling, don't you? All these people are clients of ours, too."

"I understand it's a pretty awkward situation and that if anything goes wrong it will be my fault," said Richard, on whom this fact had made a deep impression. "What can you tell me about Thorold's family?"

"A good deal, I suppose, if you're starting from scratch. What kind of thing do you want to know?"

"Everything," said Richard simply. "How they live, how many children they have, and what their financial situation is."

Bob Blake grinned at him. "That's certainly comprehensive," he said. "I'll take them in order, shall I? According to the age of the daughters, I mean."

"That would do as well as any other way," Richard assented. "One rather odd thing has struck me. Jarvis seemed to imply that they all lived in this part of the world."

"So they do."

"I should have thought one of them at least would have married a north-countryman. After all, they lived in Leeds until twenty-five years ago."

"So they did, but Thorold married late. Besides, knowing Eleanor Lawson, I should say a little bit of snobbishness had entered into it. Jock wasn't a man to drop his friends even when he'd made his pile, and the girls probably didn't know anybody they considered a fitting match."

"But that changed when they came to Hampstead?"

"It did indeed. They were married in quick succession, except Alexandra, who waited a bit. Then she took the plunge, too, with the close friend and business associate of one of her brothers-in-law, so I daresay propinquity had something to do with that. As a matter of fact, I can't help feeling that some of the men concerned may have had an eye to the main chance. Not that any of them needed money so far as I know; they all came from good families.

But you know the old saying: never marry money, but marry where money is.''

"I'll bear it in mind,'' said Richard slowly. He had his notebook out now. "Eleanor Thorold married Philip Lawson, who is a solicitor,'' he said.

"That's right. Lawson's practice is in the City, and he keeps his firm's account and his clients' account at the head-office branch here in Gracechurch Street. So I don't know anything about that, but judging from the amount they keep in the joint account at my branch, his position is pretty sound. I know Eleanor better because she's in and out all the time. A good-looking woman, but rather severe. Not affable,'' he added, evidently finding the *mot juste*.

"What about family?''

"There's just one son, also Philip, though he's generally called Phil. He's twenty-three and has just come down from university with a law degree and started to eat his dinners in one of the Inns of Court. I forget which. No going into the junior branch of the law for him.''

"That could be an expensive business. I always understood a barrister may need his family's support for years before he can fend for himself.''

"Yes, but I don't think there's any doubt they can manage it. Another thing—judging by the month-end bills that go through their personal account, they do a good deal of entertaining. That can mount up these days, as you know.''

"Yes, I know,'' said Richard with feeling. "So you think they might welcome a third of Jock's estate, rather than a quarter, but aren't in any real need of it?''

"That's it exactly. I'd say that applies to all of them. I'm a bit surprised at Philip Lawson, though; from what I have seen of him he's a fair-minded man.''

"Well, I shall know more when I've talked to him. We come to the Fieldings next, don't we?" said Richard, consulting his notes.

"Yes, and to tell you about their financial affairs I can't altogether separate them from the Bennetts. Maxwell Fielding and Wilfred Bennett have known each other all their lives as far as I know, and though they aren't in partnership they work very closely together. If Fielding gets a design job, he recommends Bennett to carry out the work. And the same thing in reverse, of course. If Bennett is building a new hospital, ten to one Fielding will be drawing up the plans."

"How nice for them," said Richard admiringly. "You seem to know a lot about their business accounts. Do they operate locally?"

"All over the country," said Blake expansively, "but Fielding's office and the head office of Bennett's firm are both in Hampstead. So I have their business accounts, as well as the private ones they keep for day-to-day expenses. A joint one in Fielding's case, but nothing like that for Wilfred Bennett. He keeps an account in his own name only and pays all the household bills himself."

"In that case, I expect you don't know Mrs. Alexandra Bennett."

"That's right. I've seen her with her husband occasionally, of course, but not to speak to."

"Do none of these women have careers of their own?"

"That's something Jock wouldn't hear of. And there's no need for it, in any case."

"We come to their families, then. The Fieldings first."

"Oh, that's a different story. They've got four children, ranging between fourteen and twenty, I should say. The two eldest are in university, and the other two, of course, still at school. I know a good deal about them because Geraldine Fielding is quite a talkative woman. There's a budding doctor among them, and one who is a disappointment because he has artistic tendencies. The younger two are girls and haven't made up their minds yet what they're going to do."

"Apart from Mrs. Fielding's confidences," said Richard, "you seem to know a great deal about all these people. How long have you been at Hampstead?"

"At the branch, ten years," said Blake, "but my family lives there so it was like going home when I took over. I got a lot of information from Jock Thorold, too. I've a feeling he was lonely and looked on me as a friend."

"And can the Fieldings manage to establish this large family in suitable professions?" Richard asked.

"Oh, I should think so. No difficulty there. In any case, I think Geraldine is bringing the two girls up to be good wives and mothers, rather old-fashioned in these days, but that's the way she sees it."

"Or the way her father saw it, from what you've told me. She may have been concerned to create a good impression."

"That's true, though I don't really believe it. But rather cynical coming from you, Richard," said Blake severely.

"The Advancement Department is a good breeding ground for cynicism," said Richard apologetically. "And have the Bennetts got an equally large family?"

"No, just one daughter. She's much younger than the others and has just started school. I think they were married about ten years before she arrived."

"And their financial situation is equally healthy?"

"Equally so."

"And still poor Mrs. Bennett hasn't got a bank account of her own and can't even sign on her husband's account."

"Yes, that's right."

"That brings us to another question, then. Was Jock Thorold generous with his daughters?"

"If you mean when they were still at home, yes, he was. And I've heard that each wedding in turn caused quite a sensation in the district, the arrangements were so lavish. But he believed very sincerely that a man should support his own wife. People said he was close with his money but I don't think it was that so much. I think he would have felt it was interfering to offer to help out."

"So none of them could look for any assistance from him if a sudden emergency arose, for instance?"

"I don't know about that. As far as I'm aware no such emergency ever arose."

"All right, then, Bob, one more question. Jarvis said you were of the opinion that Jock Thorold took this boy into his home because he had no son of his own. But from what you tell me he had three grandsons. Wasn't that enough for him?"

"I think he wanted a son, very badly. Not that he wasn't the best of fathers to his daughters, don't misunderstand me. But I have thought that perhaps...what if Malcolm Stonor was a by-blow of his? Young enough to be his grandson, but his own son in fact."

"Yes, that is a thought. Did Thorold ever hint anything of the sort to you?"

"Not a word; he could be closemouthed if he liked."

"Do you know the boy?"

"I've never had any dealings with him until recently, though I've met him when I visited the house. His allowance was only a matter of pocket money, as he still lived at home. But I have wondered.... Jock, though he was born in Yorkshire, was very proud of his Scots blood. The name young Stonor was given, Malcolm, might be an indication, if what I suspect is true.''

''Would that make any difference to this intestacy business?''

''That's something I don't know about.''

''Oh, well, I'm seeing Jake Fulford later on this afternoon; I'll ask him about it. At the time Malcolm was born, Jock Thorold was still making his periodic trips to the north?''

''Oh, yes, yes, they went on right up to the time of his accident, though, now I come to think of it, not quite so often since he took Malcolm to live with him. I'll bet,'' Blake added meditatively, ''that that's a point that was in Jarvis's mind, as well. The question of the boy's parentage,'' he explained.

2

THE OFFICES of Messrs. Fulford and Hughes, solicitors and commissioners for oaths, were in Bread Court, only a stone's throw from the block of flats where Richard and Maggie Trenton lived. Most of the Trentons' friends considered their choice of habitation eccentric, but Eden Place, built on the bombed site at the end of Bread Court, was quiet and convenient and not too expensive for a senior bank official with a growing family. So there's so much good that's come out of this unlikely commission, Richard thought as he made his way there a little later that afternoon; after his talk with Jake he could at least rely on an early arrival home.

His welcome was very different that afternoon than it had been on the occasion of his first call. Jake heard his voice in the outer office and came out himself to greet him. In the interval the men had become good friends through an occasional lunch together, though so far their families had had no dealings with each other.

Richard was a tall man himself, but Jake topped his height by at least four inches. "Come in, come in," he said, holding the door open in a welcoming way. And then, when it was closed again and Richard had taken a chair near the desk, he added with a grin, "I can look you in the face today."

"I've never noticed that you couldn't," said Richard, which was perfectly true.

"My borrowing from the bank was repaid last

week,'' said Jake impressively. "What do you think of that?''

"I take it it means that things are prospering, so of course I'm very glad to hear it." But he couldn't resist adding, "Even without that obligation outstanding, you agreed to see me."

"It's quite a serious matter," said Jake reprovingly. "Young Malcolm Stonor is a promising boy. I want to help him if I can."

"I see you're aware of the unlikely mission that's been wished on me," said Richard rather ruefully.

"Pretty well. I take it," said Jake, trying not to sound hopeful (his interests lay mainly in the criminal part of his practice), "that there's no suspicion that old Mr. Thorold was murdered?"

"Heaven forbid," said Richard piously. "Nothing like that at all. It's just a straightforward matter of seeing this Philip Lawson and trying to get him to see things a little more reasonably."

"His firm has a good reputation. Ken Hughes has had dealings with them several times. That's why I can't understand what seems to be his attitude."

"I've got all this at second hand, you know," said Richard. "We may be misjudging the man." He might have added that everything he had heard concerning the financial position of Jock Thorold's descendants was thoroughly satisfactory, but the banker's ingrained caution dies hard.

"Perhaps we are," Jake agreed. "How can I help you?"

"To begin with, what would Malcolm Stonor's position be if Lawson takes out letters of administration and only the daughters inherit?"

"If it was just a question of Malcolm's articles I'd give him them like a shot, but that was all arranged and paid for. But he has nowhere to live and nothing to live on and three years to go before his finals, and even then there's a question of a job. I talked to

Hughes about it and we've agreed to pay him for the work he does here until the five years are up, but I can't say he'll exactly be living in the lap of luxury on what he earns.''

''Where is he living now?''

''As a matter of fact he's staying with me. I gather they didn't actually tell him to get out of the Hampstead Heath house, but he felt pretty uncomfortable there.''

''Tell me, Jake, what were his expectations from Jock Thorold?''

''The old man had told him he'd see him through until he qualified, and then see him established. I think Malcolm would prefer a country practice, unless he's changed his mind and decided he likes London after all before then.''

''There's a little more to it than that,'' said Richard slowly, ''but this is in the strictest confidence. Thorold told his bank manager, whom he seems to have regarded as one of his few friends—'' He saw Fulford grinning, and broke off. ''Oh, all right, I know that's a very unnatural feeling. But it seems to have been true all the same.''

''You were going to tell me what he said to this Mr.—''

''Bob Blake. He told him, not once but several times, that he intended to leave Malcolm Stonor the factory in Leeds that was the foundation of his fortunes.''

''Yes, he'd told Malcolm that, but not at first, and to tell you the truth, Malcolm thought he wouldn't go through with it.''

''Bob thought he was quite serious. I understand Mr. Thorold had worked it out thoroughly and that it would have been a quarter of his estate, so that his three daughters each would have got a quarter themselves. So there are two questions I want to ask you. If Stonor used Blake's evidence and asked for an injunction, or whatever the right procedure would be, would he have a chance?''

"Had this Mr. Blake spoken to Thorold about making a will when he confided this to him?''

"Yes, he had, and he says Thorold expressed his intention of doing so about six months ago.''

"But apparently he never did. In that case I don't think young Malcolm would have a leg to stand on.''

"That brings me to the other question. It has been suggested that perhaps Jock Thorold took him in because Malcolm is his illegitimate son. Would that make any difference?''

"If it could be proved, certainly it would,'' Jake said slowly. "There was the Act of 1969, and a case some years later, I can't quite remember when, that established that being born a bastard hardly made any difference in property rights—or the right to succeed on intestacy—considering the general attitude toward illegitimacy these days.'' He had obviously been racking his memory as he spoke, but he paused there and then said more naturally, "That's all very well, but Malcolm has never said a word to me to indicate that that might be the case. Nor did Thorold when the original arrangements for his articles were made. And when I heard the position that had arisen following the old man's death I made a point of getting hold of a copy of Malcolm's birth certificate.''

"So the idea wasn't quite strange to you? Well, I should have expected that. Did it tell you anything?''

"Only that we must presume him to be illegitimate. The father's name was not given—that isn't obligatory, you know.''

"I didn't know, but I should like to talk to Stonor, if you don't mind. If I can learn anything about his past that might be . . . well, let's say suggestive, it might be an added shot in my locker when I talk to Lawson.''

"Yes, I see what you mean. You know, Richard, I don't envy you that talk at all."

"The way it was put to me I didn't have much choice," Richard assured him. "Has Stonor ever talked to you about his past?"

"No, for a rather talkative young man he's been strangely reticent on the subject. Shall we see if he is more willing to talk to you?"

"I shan't mention anything about the possible larger legacy that Thorold intended," said Richard hastily. "You say it was mentioned to him, but his attitude seems to be the sensible one and in the circumstances it's best forgotten. I shall take it up with Lawson, of course, but I think we'll have to be content with just getting the boy established in life, if that's at all possible. It would be unkind to raise any false hopes."

"Oh, I agree with you there," said Fulford emphatically. "Do you mind if I sit in on your talk, Richard? I'll send for Malcolm to come in here if that's all right with you."

"Yes, of course it is."

Jake spoke into the telephone. "I don't suppose he'll be more than a moment," he said, replacing the receiver.

II

IT WAS, however, a few minutes before the office boy could find Malcolm Stonor, and when he came in he had a bunch of papers in his hand, a worried look and hair rather disordered. "I couldn't quite finish that abstract, Mr. Fulford," he said apologetically. "Were you wanting it urgently?" Then he saw Richard. "Oh, I'm sorry, I thought—"

"It's all right, Malcolm, come in," said Jake.

"This is Mr. Trenton, who is at the head office of the Northumberland and Wessex Bank. He's going to try to make Mr. Lawson see reason about the family continuing your allowance until you qualify."

Malcolm Stonor was a well-built youngster, not very tall, with sandy hair and a formidable pair of horn-rimmed spectacles. He turned politely to Richard. "Good afternoon, Mr. Trenton," he said. "It's awfully good of you to bother, but I don't see there's any reason in the world why they should care what happens to me. Or why the bank should care, either," he added frowning.

"Let's say a sense of fair play comes into it," said Jake hastily, for which Richard was grateful. It saved him skirting round the subject of what he felt the general managers' real motives were.

"But I can't do anything without your help, Mr. Stonor," he said formally.

"Well, of course, I'd help you if I could, but I don't see—"

"I'd like to know something about you," said Richard simply.

"There's nothing really to know. I'm endlessly grateful to Mr. Thorold, but I don't want to—to impose upon the family now that he's dead."

"What do you propose to do, then?" asked Richard, genuinely curious to hear the young man's version of what Jake had arranged.

"Mr. Fulford has promised to pay me while I finish my articles, just as though I were employed in the ordinary way. I can't tell you how grateful I am to him for that. But I'm not worth an awful lot yet, you know, and it's going to be difficult. And I can't say I like taking what's more or less charity." Jake shook his head at that, but didn't interrupt. Malcolm paused there and then said in a rush, "I suppose you're thinking that's exactly what happened when Mr. Thorold took me in. But it wasn't quite the same, it was his own choice. Mr. Fulford, and Mr. Hughes, of course, have more or less had me wished on them now.''

"Yes, I do see the difference," said Richard quietly. "And if I can help, I will. I'm going to ask you some questions now, personal questions, and maybe you won't like them." He paused and smiled at Malcolm. "Will you bear in mind that I mean well?" he said.

That brought an answering smile. "The way to hell—" said Stonor, and didn't attempt to complete the quotation. "Should we go to my room, Mr. Fulford? Are we disturbing you?"

"Not a bit, I'll be glad to hear what you have to say—if you don't mind my being present," said Jake formally.

"Then we'll go right back to the beginning," said Richard firmly, not waiting for Malcolm's agreement but taking it for granted. "Where were you born and who were your parents? And for heaven's sake," he added almost irritably, "sit down and relax a little."

"All right." Malcolm obeyed, though rather gingerly, and perched himself on the edge of one of the visitors' chairs. Jake reached out a hand and took the papers that he was clutching from him and began to glance through them as though dissociating himself from the whole affair. Richard thought he could assess the other man's feelings well enough: he was interested in hearing what Malcolm had to say but sensitive enough to realize that it is sometimes more difficult to talk with a third person present.

"I was born in Leeds," said Stonor promptly. "In one of the hospitals, I suppose, though I don't remember my mother ever pointing out to me which it was. She wasn't a sentimental woman. We lived as

long as I remember in one of the terrace houses near
the Tam O'Shanter Clothing factory, where she was
employed. She worked one of the machines. In fact,
I think she spent her whole life fitting right sleeves
into jackets—the woman next to her did the left
ones—which I imagine must have been pretty bor-
ing, though she used to laugh about it sometimes
and say that except for giving the lapels a good fit it
was the most important job in the place. It was a far
cry from Pleasant Street to Hampstead Heath, I can
tell you,'' he added inconsequently. "Did you
know, Mr. Trenton, that in the north of England,
streets called Pleasant—there are four of them that
I know of in Leeds alone—are always particularly
shoddy?''

"No, I didn't know that. You're saying the surroundings you grew up in weren't particularly
nice.''

"Not judged by the standards I've been acquiring
for the past five years,'' said Malcolm. "A parlor, a
kitchen, a scullery at the back, which we also used
as a bathroom—and by that I don't mean there was
a bath there, just that it was the most convenient
place to wash—and two bedrooms upstairs. Everything was kept spotlessly clean—that applied to the
whole street as a matter of fact. It was just that,
outside, the houses were a grimy-looking gray. But
it was the rare housewife who didn't have clean
curtains at a well-polished window, and of course
the doorsteps were donkeystoned—''

"What on earth is that?'' asked Richard, the Lon-
doner.

"Well,'' said Malcolm doubtfully (he had obviously never considered the matter before), "I just
mean they were whitened, or most of them. And
that had to be done every morning, because, of
course, as soon as you went into the house there
were footmarks again. And I'm not really meaning

to complain about any undue hardship; please don't think that for a moment. At the time, what have come to seem rather cramped quarters were perfectly natural to me. And we never lacked for anything material, clothes or food, and there was always the library for books. I did rather well in my eleven plus, so I was able to go to grammar school. Some of the boys there came from families that were much better off, and I never felt out of the way by being extraordinarily shabby or anything like that. It's only later that I've wondered how mum managed it on her wages.''

"Your father?'' said Richard, making the words a question.

"She said he died when I was three months old,'' said Malcolm doubtfully, "and she called herself Mrs. Stonor. It was only later I wondered about that. . . I suppose not until I was ten or eleven years old, which you may think was a little dim of me. You see, there wasn't a single picture of him in the house anywhere; she never told me what he did for a living, or how he died, or anything. When it did occur to me that that was a little odd, of course I began to ask questions, but she always evaded them, and if she couldn't do that she snapped at me to be quiet and not worry her. That wasn't like mum; she was a good sort, always cheerful.''

"You may have decided that Mr. Stonor was mythical,'' Richard pointed out, "but I'm sure you gave more thought to the matter as you grew older.''

"Well, I did. I decided I was a bastard,'' said Malcolm defiantly. "That's the right legal term, isn't it?'' he added, turning to Jake.

"It will do as well as another,'' said Jake mildly. "But I think Mr. Trenton would like to know—and so should I, of course—whether you could produce any evidence to support that point of view.''

"There were . . . things," Malcolm admitted.

"What sort of things?"

He looked appealingly from one of them to the other. "Is all this really necessary?" he asked.

"I don't need to tell you that what used to be regarded as the stain of illegitimacy is no longer so looked down on in this permissive age," said Jake carefully. "Similarly, from your mother's point of view—"

"That's just it," Malcolm burst out. "She brought me up . . . . well, I suppose you'd say to be straitlaced about these things. That's why it seems so dreadful to be saying—to be even thinking—these things about her."

"Your mother was a Yorkshire woman," said Richard, coming back into the conversation.

"Yes, she was."

"Then I'm sure she'd have told you to tell the truth and shame the devil, if the question ever arose."

Malcolm thought that out for a moment and smiled. "I expect she would," he said and allowed his accent to broaden. "Get on with it, then, lad, tell the man what he wants to know."

"I'm beginning to like your mother," said Richard truthfully.

"Oh, you would have done." He paused for a moment, obviously considering the story he was to tell and not terribly happy about it. "Well, you see," he said at last, "there were times, when I was little, she'd bundle me off to a neighbor and I wouldn't see her for a day or two. But by the time I was eight or so she said I was old enough to look after myself, and so I was, of course. She always saw there was plenty to eat, things I could make for myself quite easily. And money for fish and chips, too. So later I wondered . . . I'm not saying I blamed her, you know; it was quite natural she wanted a man from time to time, and she always took great care to keep me out of it."

"So you think you were the outcome of some such chance encounter?" said Richard. It never occurred to him that it was odd that Malcolm should be unburdening himself to him like this; people always did if they got the opportunity, and he considered it quite natural.

"Well, I suppose I must be, don't you?"

"I think we'll leave that question for the moment. Your mother died five years ago, I believe." His tone was sympathetic, and Malcolm responded at once.

"Yes, she did, and she was ill the whole winter before she died. Not in hospital, I mean, at home. I did what I could to look after her, and the district nurse came in. They said it was cancer and it was too widespread to operate. That was just like mum; she would never consider herself, and if she felt ill she'd do her best to hide it from everyone."

"You were fifteen at the time," said Richard—a statement this time, not a question.

"Fifteen when she died," said Malcolm precisely. "Everyone was kind. I don't know how I'd have got on without the neighbors."

"No, I can imagine that. But I'm wondering how you lived during those . . . six months, did you say?"

"Why, her money from the factory kept on coming. There's no mystery about that."

"I see. And at what point did Mr. Thorold come into the picture?"

"When she was first ill and away from work he came to see her. She'd been with the factory for twenty-five years and they all thought the world of her. He wasn't living in Leeds then, you know, but he made frequent visits—still did all the time I lived with him, though not quite so often, I think. So he'd turn up at the house about once a month while she was ill with some flowers and some books—she was a great reader, mum was. So I wasn't surprised to see him at the funeral, and he came back to the house afterward, and after everyone else had gone he said he'd like to take me to live with him.''

"And what had you to say to that?" Even as a boy it was unlikely Malcolm would have jumped at the opportunity without examining it carefully from all sides first.

"I think you can imagine, I was flummoxed," said Malcolm. "I hadn't got to the state of thinking what I'd do: mum had no relatives, you see, so I was quite alone in the world. I supposed there would be social workers, people like that, but. . .oh, I was too miserable after mum died to think about it at all.''

"Tell me about your talk with Jock Thorold."

"It was an odd business really. First he told me the local authorities were quite willing for him to take over my guardianship. That didn't surprise me. He was well-known locally. . .a man of substance, you might say. But then he was very concerned to point out the difficulties ahead if I took him up on his offer. He'd send me to a public school—not one of the ones you have to have your name down at birth for, of course—and see me through the training for whatever profession I chose. But there'd be people who resented my good fortune, and still more who'd look down on my background, I must remember that."

"That didn't frighten you?"

Malcolm grinned again. "I was terrified," he admitted. "But I'd got to like him, you know. That was quite genuine, not cupboard love or anything like that. And though he didn't say so, I had a feeling he was lonely. So I asked him if he'd let me think it over, and then next day I said yes."

"He never mentioned the question of formal adoption?"

"Well, in passing, but that was later. He said it would be rather silly at my age, and quite unnecessary, as he would look after me just as he'd promised. It was rather a facer when he died. But it was like mum's death: I was too upset to be thinking about material things for a while. Until I was forced to when it became obvious I wasn't welcome at the house anymore."

"You'd expected, I suppose, to be included in his will."

"I never even thought about it, and I daresay that seems strange to you, since the law is my chosen career. He always looked so healthy, I didn't think he'd die yet. And I knew I could look after myself once I was through my finals."

"Tell me about your life with him, then."

"It was just as he said: going to school was pretty grim at first. Not that I ever told him that. Even though I'd accepted what he offered, I still had a certain amount of pride in trying to stand on my own feet." He paused there and his voice became tinged with enthusiasm. "He was a great old boy, you know, always game for anything. We spent a lot of time together during the school holidays, but he was always very careful not to make me feel I owed him anything. And it wasn't that, really; I liked being with him. And since I left school and came here we'd see even more of each other, because I went home every night. Of course, as I daresay you know, there's a lot of studying to do, but he knew I was there if he wanted me. The only snag during the whole five years I was with him was the attitude of the family."

"Yes, I thought we should come to them before long."

"I suppose you want me to tell you—"

"I'm afraid I do."

"Well, the three girls were quite different from

their father. Jock was a down-to-earth chap. I don't think all the money he'd made ever changed him a jot from what he'd been originally. His daughters had all married well, and I think regarded themselves as having gone up in the world. Well, I suppose that was true. But they didn't like him coming home with a factory worker's son in tow, and I can see their point about that, you know. Anyway, they all said what they thought in turn in no uncertain manner. No, I should except Mrs. Bennett—that's Alexandra, the youngest daughter; in her case I think it was her husband who saw me as a threat."

"That was the cause of the trouble, then? They thought Mr. Thorold's estate might have to be divided four ways instead of three?"

"I think that crossed their minds, or something like it. But it wasn't only that." He paused there, cogitating. "Or perhaps it was," he said then, slowly. "I really don't know."

"Did Mr. Thorold tell you about his family's attitude?"

"No, not a word. Neither did they until after he died, though the atmosphere was always extremely chilly. But I heard an absolutely monumental row going on only minutes after we got to the house that first day."

"Could you explain that a little further?"

"Yes, Mrs. Lawson was there. That's Eleanor, the eldest daughter. Of course, it must have been a shock to her. She came into the hall when she heard her father's key in the lock, and there he was with me, as well. And that was the first, quite obviously, that she had known about the arrangement. Jock took one look at her and said, 'Wait for me in the drawing room, Eleanor,' and took me upstairs himself and showed me my room and told me to make myself comfortable. He'd call me when he was ready." There came another of those pauses. "I'm not really very proud of what I did then, and I did wait long enough to unpack my suitcase, though that didn't take much doing. But then I just had to find out what was happening, and I went downstairs. There was nobody about but I could hear voices from the room on the right of the hall. Jock was saying, more patiently than I'd have expected from what I knew of him later, 'He's a good boy and a clever boy, and I think I can make something of him. Have you any objection to that?' And Mrs. Lawson went into a sort of tirade in reply, talking about her son, Phil: 'If you want a male heir, isn't he enough for you?' And Jock just replied quietly, 'Has Phil ever wanted for anything in his life? I should have thought your husband was quite capable of supporting his family.' So then she changed her tack and asked, 'Who is this boy, anyway?' And all Jock would say—and he sounded amused—was, 'A Yorkshire tyke, just like you are, lass.' And that made her angrier than ever.''

''Was that all?''

''No, they went on and on. But the same things over and over. At last I heard someone coming from the back of the hall, so I nipped upstairs again. And I never said anything to Jock about what I'd heard, and he never said anything to me.''

''Did you overhear any further remonstrances from the members of the family?''

''No, I didn't.''

''Then for all you know, Mrs. Lawson may be the only one who objected to your presence.''

''I don't think that's the case,'' said Malcolm doubtfully. ''They all came regularly for Sunday dinner, which Jock still insisted on having at midday. The three daughters, their husbands and all the children—except when they were away at school or university, of course. Those were uncomfortable occasions, I can tell you. I didn't enjoy them a bit. You could have cut the atmosphere with a knife. I think they all hated me.''

"What happened after Mr. Thorold died?''

"That was only the beginning of last week,'' said Malcolm in a wondering tone. "It seems as if it was forever. It never occurred to me to do anything but go on as usual. Anyway, I still had some of my quarter's allowance left. But after the funeral Philip Lawson took me to one side and said that the family didn't think it suitable for me to stay on in the Hampstead house. It was going to be sold. And I'm afraid I just stared at him, not really thinking anybody would be making plans so soon. Only then he said, 'You must realize, Malcolm, that you have no claim on the family, and your benefactor died intestate. It will be up to you to make your own arrangements from now on.' So there was nothing else to do. I packed my bags—I'd rather more things to bring with me this time—and came to the office to ask Mr. Fulford's advice. He quite agreed it was out of the question for me to do anything myself about staying on in Hampstead, and I'm in his spare room at the moment. But I've got to find somewhere of my own, of course.''

"I've got an idea about that,'' said Richard. "There are some studio flats on the ground floor of Eden Place, where I live, and I think one of them has just come empty. If you like, I'll talk to the landlord.''

"Would you? That's just at the end of the court, isn't it? I'd save on fares that way.''

"Exactly what I had in mind. I'll see what I can do, Malcolm, and in any case I shall be reporting back to you and Mr. Fulford about my talk with Philip Lawson later today.''

"Is that all for the moment, then?'' Malcolm got up as he spoke and held out his hand for the papers, which were now lying on the desk in front of Jake

Fulford. "I can't say I've enjoyed our talk, Mr. Trenton," he added, smiling to take any sting out of the words, "but I do realize you're undertaking a very awkward job for me and I'm grateful, though I don't think it will be the slightest use."

3

"I DIDN'T KNOW you concerned yourself with such mundane matters as conveyancing," said Richard idly as the door closed behind Stonor.

"I don't," said Jake. "Ken Hughes has been out with one of those summer colds, and though he's back in his office now he's way behind in his work. And I'd prefer something more lively, but I haven't forgotten everything I learned."

"No, of course not. How did young Stonor's story strike you, Jake?"

"As it did you, I expect. I think he's got the idea that his mother was promiscuous, but she doesn't sound like that sort to me."

"Nor to me. Do you think these disappearances of hers coincided with the times that Jock Thorold was in Leeds?"

"I should think it very likely myself. A long-term attachment like that would be quite a different matter from her point of view. And then there's the fact that Malcolm says they never wanted for anything, and that his mother's wages were paid all the time she was ill. I don't think it would be normal for a factory worker to go on being paid for six months."

"Then you agree that Malcolm is probably Thorold's son? If that could be proved—"

"Yes, but can it?"

"We could try. Anyway, I don't see any harm in hinting at the possibility to Mr. Lawson when I talk

to him. That might induce a little more reasonable
attitude. He wouldn't want the matter dragged out
in court, and he'd know that if it were, some provision would be made for the boy.''

"That sounds suspiciously like blackmail to me,
Richard,'' said Jake in an amused tone.

"Nothing of the sort. Merely pointing out possibil-
ities. Let's work out a timetable, Jake. Malcolm said
his mother went to work at the factory about
twenty-five years ago; that must have been just
about the time Jock left Leeds and came to Hampstead.''

"If that's right, then we're assuming that he met
her on one of his later trips. Malcolm is twenty, but
we don't know how long the affaire had been going
on before he was born. I say,'' said Jake, his legal
caution suddenly getting the better of him, ''we're
making an awful lot of assumptions, aren't we?''

"I don't think they're altogether unjustified,''
said Richard slowly. ''Anyway, the affaire, if
there was an affaire,'' he added in deference to his
companion, ''seems to have lasted until Mrs.
Stonor's death. In the meantime he'd obviously
been helping out; I don't see him as a man to shirk
his obligations. And then he took the boy home
with him. I wonder what arguments he used to
make Malcolm agree; he strikes me as an independent sort of chap.''

"I think it most likely occurred to him, just as it
has done to us, that he probably is Jock Thorold's
natural son—though not, perhaps, that the liaison
had been going on for over twenty years. In which
case he takes a rather more charitable view of his
half sisters' attitude than you might expect. Still. . .
what are your plans now, Richard?''

"I have an appointment with Philip Lawson
about ten tomorrow morning. If you like we can
have lunch together and I'll tell you what he says.''

"That will suit me fine.''

"But just now," added Richard firmly, getting to his feet, "I'm going home to have tea with my wife, and I'm going to forget all about Jock Thorold's affairs."

II

IF RICHARD REALLY THOUGHT THIS he was the more deceived. Strolling down Bread Court toward Eden Place, where he lived with his wife, Maggie, he saw ahead of him his young son, Ricky. Ricky was nine now, the only one of the children at home, his elder brother and sister, Hugh and Jane, being still several weeks away from the end of the summer term at their respective boarding schools. Ricky at present attended a rather progressive private school, it being the only one available locally, which sometimes worried his father, until Richard concluded the boy would soon have any nonsense knocked out of him when he joined Hugh at his prep school. By then, of course, he remembered, Hugh would have gone on to public school, but the principle was the same.

"Wait for me, Ricky," he called as soon as he came within earshot.

"Daddy!" Ricky whirled when he heard his father's voice. "What are you doing here so early? You're never here at this time of day." And then, light suddenly dawning, "You've been to see Mr. Fulford about another case, and so you came straight home. Is something up?"

"Nothing's up," said Richard rather dampeningly, for which he may be excused. Twice in the past Ricky had cast his father for the role of the Great Detective, for which he felt himself singularly inadequate, and the slightest deviation from normal was apt to set Ricky off again. "I *have* been to see Mr. Fulford—a matter of business connected with the bank. And you know I like him; we chatted for a while."

"I'd like to meet him," said Ricky, falling into step beside his father. In a way, that is; actually he was hopping on one foot. "But I heard you say once he has a criminal practice. Has one of your customers been breaking the law?"

"Nothing like that. A very simple matter . . . and confidential," said Richard, hoping that would close the matter. But when he got upstairs he found that Maggie was almost as inquisitive as her son; she didn't actually ask questions but she looked them. Hours of business in the Advance Department were apt to be pretty regular, so she was as surprised as Ricky to see her husband home so early.

However, she said obligingly, "Tea's ready in the kitchen, Ricky. I'll bring ours into the living room, shall I, Richard?"

"That would be a good idea," said Richard, following her into the kitchen. He thought it would be a good idea to make sure the boy was really settled down. "What on earth is that?" he added, stopping on the threshold. There was a picture stuck up on the door of the refrigerator, a blinding conglomeration of all the primary colors, and a few invented ones, as well.

"I thought you'd like it," said Ricky complacently. "It's for Jane."

"There isn't an inch of room left in her bedroom," Richard objected.

"No, for school."

"You gave her a painting for Christmas. The headmistress may not like too much decoration in the bedrooms."

"She won't mind this," said Ricky. "It's a religious painting."

"Is it?" asked his father, stunned.

"Yes, they set us to do it at school in art class," said Ricky. "But it's finished, so I brought it home at lunchtime."

"What is it?"

"Can't you see? I should have thought it was obvious," said Ricky in a very superior tone. "The flight into Egypt."

"Oh, yes, of course." Original as ever, Ricky had painted a yellow donkey, a Madonna in scarlet and a St. Joseph with ginger hair and a robe of shocking pink. The baby wore green, and they were obviously crossing a sandy tract of desert. "Very nice indeed," said Richard weakly.

"There, you see!" said Ricky triumphantly to his mother. "And I ought to tell you, daddy, it was the best one in the class. Do you know that Pete Watkins just put a dot in the middle of the paper, but he doesn't really like painting and isn't much good at it."

"A dot? What was that supposed to represent?"

"The flea!" said Ricky, and burst into laughter. "Take the child and the mother and flea into Egypt," he quoted. "Don't you think that's terribly funny?"

"Oh, yes, I do," said Richard obligingly. "But I didn't know anybody at the school had any religious beliefs at all," he added to Maggie as they left their son to an ample repast, guaranteed to keep him quiet for at least ten minutes.

"They don't," Maggie agreed, "but the art mistress is temporary, I think. And you mustn't discourage him, darling; he may be a great artist someday."

"He may," said Richard, putting down the tray and flinging himself into his favorite armchair. He regarded his wife with satisfaction. Maggie had a mop of red curls and a creamy complexion, not exactly conventionally good-looking but beautiful in his eyes. When she was wearing heels she was nearly as tall as he was himself, and for her height was certainly thinner than she should be; there was also no doubt that she could be on occasion a worrier, as was evidenced by her anxious expression now.

"Darling Richard," she said, "what is it this time?"

Richard sat up again, straighter than the chair would comfortably allow. "What makes you think that anything is up?" he demanded.

"Your expression," said Maggie, taking time to answer him accurately, "and I think you've been snubbing Ricky, haven't you? I admit he does ask too many questions."

"And you don't ask any at all," said Richard, teasing her, and sinking back into his chair again.

"Not until you want me to," said Maggie simply. "And if you ask me, Richard, you're bursting to tell me something or other."

He knew from long experience that she was absolutely trustworthy. "I think Ricky is hoping for another murder, but there's nothing like that at all. However, I may as well tell you." He started with his talk with Jarvis that morning and went on to the final discussion with Jake Fulford a short while before.

"I don't think it was very nice of Mr. Thorold to leave things in such a muddle," said Maggie rather severely. "He's got that poor boy used to a good life now; he should never have left him up in the air like this."

"Young Stonor doesn't seem to look at it that way. He's grateful for the chance he's being given in life and quite willing to take responsibility for himself now. I must say, Maggie, I like the boy."

"But the family! Richard, I'm so sorry you have to see that horrible man tomorrow."

"We don't know that he *is* horrible, Maggie. He may be a nice chap. In fact, though Bob Blake doesn't know him well, he's always considered him a fair-minded man, he says."

"He seems to me to be contradicting himself,"
said Maggie. "If Mr. Lawson is really fair-minded
there wouldn't be any need for you to go to see him
at all."

"I don't think that follows. He's only an in-law
after all. It's the three daughters who would be doing the inheriting, and I imagine he has to comply
with their wishes."

"Then perhaps it's them you ought to be seeing,"
said Maggie, lucidly if ungrammatically.

"It's already occurred to me that I might talk to
Mrs. Lawson. I don't know if there's any point in
going further than that. Anyway, Maggie, you can
see for yourself it is only a formality, nothing to
worry about. Even Malcolm doesn't expect anything to come of it."

"Do you want me to see if that studio downstairs
is still vacant, and phone Jake Fulford about it?"

"I wish you would." But Maggie was still frowning and he added rather impatiently, "I told you
there was nothing to worry about."

"I'm just wondering," said Maggie, "what exactly *is* the bank's angle in all this?"

"Bob Blake's point of view is quite simple: he
looked on Jock Thorold as a friend and wants to do
what he wished."

"You mean, to persuade Mr. Lawson that Malcolm ought to inherit the factory?"

"It isn't exactly up to him. Well, I'd have to ask
Jake what the prodecure is. All I know is Philip
Lawson is the obvious person to apply for letters of
administration. There isn't a chance of allotting the
factory to Malcolm, Maggie, and I think Bob realizes
it. All we can possibly do is get him seen comfortably through his articles, and with a bit of luck, perhaps, have a little money provided to buy him into a
practice."

"Malcolm could apply to the court, couldn't he? I

don't know the procedure, either, but surely there
must be some way.''

"According to Jake he might have some hope if
he could prove he was actually Jock Thorold's son.
Without such proof. . . but in any case, I don't think
Malcolm *would* take action. As I said, his main feeling toward Mr. Thorold is one of gratitude.''

"I can see you sympathize with Bob," said Maggie, who didn't seem to have been listening, "because it's how any decent person would feel—"

"Any decent person who wasn't a member of the
family perhaps," said Richard. "It might be fairer
to put it that way."

"I don't think that I much care about being fair to
people like that," Maggie told him. "How much is
the estate worth anyway?''

"I don't know. Lawson may be able to tell me."

"Anyway, you're distracting me from my question. I understand Bob Blake's feelings, and I
understand yours, though I wish you thought you
could do more for Malcolm Stonor. But what about
Mr. Jarvis?''

"If anything turns up, if a will is found after all,
for instance, or if the family relents and decides to
cut him in on the deal," said Richard, "the bank
would want to stand well with a possible future
client who would be a very wealthy young man."

"How horribly cynical! You mean they think he
might take the account away from whichever of
your branches it's in unless you try to help him
now?''

"Something like that," Richard agreed. But at
that moment, and rather to his relief, Ricky burst
into the room to announce that he had finished his
tea.

"And you must have been talking an awful lot,"
he added accusingly, eyeing the two full cups that
Maggie had poured and both of them had forgotten

to touch. "I think it's really mean of you, daddy, not to tell me if you're helping the police again."

"The police have nothing to do with this," said Richard, and perhaps the heartfelt nature of the remark went a good way toward convincing his son of the truth of what he was saying. "That," he added, looking at Maggie for sympathy, "would be just about the last straw."

4

As Bob Blake had said, Philip Lawson's office was in the City. Richard's appointment was for ten o'clock the following morning. He arrived in good time and was pleasantly surprised not to be kept waiting. The suite of offices, in one of the newer buildings, was just about as different from Fulford and Hughes's rather Dickensian quarters as could possibly be imagined, and Lawson's office, in defiance of all tradition, definitely in the luxury class. No spiders lurking in the corners, and sparkling clean windows, so that Richard was reminded of Malcolm Stonor's description of his humble abode in one of the Pleasant streets in Leeds. Lawson himself was a tall, well-built man with a rugged complexion, who looked as if he would be more comfortable in country clothes than in the traditional city garb he had chosen to wear. He greeted Richard affably and without surprise, though it was immediately apparent that he had no idea at all of the reason for the visit. "It's good of you to take the trouble to come," he said, "and if the occasion arises, of course, I shall call on your Trustee Department's services. But at the moment, dealing with my father-in-law's estate is really quite a simple matter." He smiled as though some thought pleased him and then added, "Large or small, it's all the same really."

"I wonder if you know why I'm here, Mr. Lawson," said Richard, speaking rather more tentatively than was customary with him.

"I had a telephone call from a Mr. Jarvis, who I understand is one of the joint general managers of the bank. He said you would be coming to see me to-day and I assumed—"

"I'm not from the Trustee Department, Mr. Lawson."

"Aren't you? Then I don't quite see what business we can have together."

"Actually I work in the Advance Department, but—"

"Don't tell me Jock muddled things. There was absolutely no need for him to be overdrawn."

"No, that's not it. I was about to add, that's nothing to do with my visit, either. It was merely," he added ruefully, and perhaps a little too frankly, "that I had the bad luck to be selected for a rather delicate task."

"If I said, I see, I should be lying," said Lawson, eyeing him curiously. "What can my affairs, or my father-in-law's or my wife's or any of the other members of her family, possibly have to do with you?"

"It's a question about Mr. Thorold's protégé, Malcolm Stonor," Richard explained. As he spoke he knew that the statement was too bald, that he should have approached the matter more obliquely, but it wasn't easy to think how this might have been done.

"What about Malcolm?" Lawson's tone had sharpened. "Old Jock died intestate, did you know that? And Stonor, not being a member of the family, can claim no share in the estate."

"Are you so sure about that? About Mr. Thorold dying intestate, I mean."

"Sure enough. I acted as his solicitor, you know. If he'd wanted to make a will he'd have come to me."

"Perhaps if he was about to do something of which he knew you'd disapprove—"

"I should have been bound to follow his instructions, of course. In any case, his death has been widely publicized. I think there's no question that if he had been to another solicitor we should have heard by now. Besides that, the house has been searched. There's neither an original nor a copy there."

"Yes, I suppose if there had been a will you'd have been bound to know by now. Did you never represent to him the desirability of making one?"

"Yes, of course I did. I would have been failing in my duty not to do so. He always said there was time enough, and I'm afraid I was deceived into thinking so, too. He gave the impression of being quite indestructible."

"I can understand in your particular circumstances—"

"If you mean because Eleanor will inherit—" said Lawson rather quickly. "If old Jock *had* made a will it might not have worked out quite like that. I don't mean he'd have disinherited her; he had too much of a sense of justice for that. But his youngest daughter, Alex, was always his favorite. In any case, I assure you that didn't prevent me from advising him to the best of my ability."

"No, I'm sure it didn't." Richard was quite genuine in saying that; he felt it must be true. "Was there no discussion on the subject, though? Just your suggestion and a flat refusal?"

"That was it, more or less. I explained to him the complications of dying intestate, but as I say, he didn't seem to think that would arise."

"You yourself will be applying for letters of administration?"

"Yes, certainly. Max and Wilfred—that's Fielding and Bennett, my wife's brothers-in-law—neither of them wants the bother, and anyway, it seems to be natural for me to do so. I have the agreement of the whole family, but in case you're wondering what will happen after that, Mr. Trenton, I am bound to distribute the estate in strict accordance with the laws of intestacy."

Richard hesitated, but the question had to be asked sooner or later. "Did Mr. Thorold ever mention making any provision for Malcolm Stonor?" he asked.

For the first time Philip Lawson seemed a little uneasy. "He said nothing to me," he said, "but I always believed it was his intention to do so. And truth to tell, I'd like to see something done for the boy."

"Couldn't it at least be arranged for his allowance to continue until he has finished his articles?"

"Not without the consent of the beneficiaries." Lawson, too, hesitated. "I see I must be frank with you, Mr. Trenton," he said uncomfortably. "My wife and her sisters are not in perfect agreement on all points, but on this point they're unanimous. They disapproved of their father taking Malcolm in and are quite adamant that nothing shall be done for him now. This is a matter, of course, on which I must defer to their wishes. I only come into it at second hand."

"Yes, I see that, but I don't understand it," said Richard frankly. "I've been told that the estate is a very large one."

"It is indeed, though I can't give you any details at the moment. But forgive me, Mr. Trenton, I find all this rather puzzling. What exactly is your concern with Malcolm?"

"There was one person with whom Jock Thorold was rather more frank about his intentions than he was with you, Mr. Lawson. I can understand that, in view of what you tell me; I take it there's some family feeling involved. But he spoke to the manager of our Hampstead branch, Mr. Robert Blake, and I should tell you that his intentions toward young Stonor were extremely generous. Unfortunately, in that case, too, he said he had time enough to think about making his will later."

"Yes, I can understand your concern better now. Perhaps you would be kind enough to tell me exactly what Jock said to Mr. Blake. I believe my wife knows him better than I do," he added thoughtfully. "We have only our personal account at that branch, you know, but I've always regarded him as a responsible person."

Richard ventured a grin at that. "Hampstead is an important branch," he said. "He wouldn't be there if he weren't responsible."

"No, I can see that." Lawson returned the smile. "Do you mind telling me, though—"

"What Mr. Thorold told him? No, that's really what I came here to do. It was his intention, he said, to leave Malcolm Stonor the Tam O'Shanter Clothing factory in Leeds. From what he also said, I think Blake got the impression that that represented about one quarter of his estate."

Philip Lawson thought about that for a while. "I daresay that's true enough," he said. "And I hope you see—" he laughed unwillingly "—that you're putting me in a very uncomfortable position, Mr. Trenton."

"I'm sorry for that," said Richard. "I might add that Stonor himself is making no complaint; he feels he has been treated with great generosity already. But I think you'll agree that the request I'm making on his behalf is an extremely moderate one in the circumstances."

"Had Jock told him about this possibility?"

"Yes, but not until fairly recently. Until then he was under the impression that Mr. Thorold intended to educate him and see him through until he qualified. Mr. Fulford, one of the partners in the firm with which he's articled, was also told there'd be money to buy him a partnership. But I felt you were entitled to the whole story.''

"Certainly, I agree with you. Would you ask Mr. Blake to write all this down for me, as clearly as he can. I'd like to show his letter to my wife and to Mrs. Fielding and Mrs. Bennett.''

"Of course I'll do that. But do you think it will make any difference?''

Lawson laughed again. Richard thought he had never heard anyone who sounded less amused. "No, I don't," he said positively. "Eleanor is quite adamant: Malcolm was an interloper and deserves nothing at all from the family.''

"And Mr. Thorold's other two daughters?''

"I've only got their opinions at second hand through my wife. I gather they're the same as hers. You must understand, Mr. Trenton, when Jock came back from Leeds five years ago bringing the boy with him it was a tremendous shock to all of them.''

"Stonor had never been mentioned to them before?''

"Not a word. Eleanor happened to be at Jock's house when the two of them arrived; otherwise the first any of us knew of it would have been when Malcolm was already in residence there. I hope you'll agree with me, Mr. Trenton, because I think that if Jock had been a little more tactful their attitude might have been very different. But then, you know, there's the maternal instinct. There are grandchildren, too.''

"Yes, I understood that from Mr. Blake.''

"Phil's all right, that's my son. He's going to be a barrister, and I understand there are some lean years ahead of him. I can see him through that all right, but you'd never get Eleanor to look at it that way.''

That was a matter upon which Richard didn't feel himself competent to comment. "What do you know of the circumstances of Stonor's adoption? That's the wrong word, I know; if it were the right one things would be a lot easier. But I was wondering what Mr. Thorold told you."

"Not a word. In his own way I suppose he was a bit of an autocrat. What he'd done he'd done, and that should be enough for the rest of us."

"He gave up full control of the factory twenty-five years ago, when he came south," said Richard.

"So I've been told."

"And since then he made frequent visits north, to see that things were going well, I suppose."

"Yes, he wasn't one to trust things altogether to others. I'd say he went up once a month on an average, though not quite so often after he brought Malcolm here."

"Malcolm's mother, Lilian Stonor, went to work at the factory about twenty-five years ago," said Richard. "Malcolm himself is twenty years old, I believe. As long as he remembers, his mother was in the habit of leaving home for two or three days at a time on occasion, though until he was eight years old, when she felt he should be capable of looking after himself, she always made arrangements for a neighbor to take him in. During Mrs. Stonor's last illness—she called herself that, though Malcolm has no knowledge of his father and his birth certificate gives only his mother's name—Mr. Thorold was a frequent visitor. He went to the funeral, and then suggested to Malcolm that he should come back to London with him. He was quite open about the difficulties the boy would encounter in adjusting to a new environment, and to tell you the truth, I'm not quite sure how he persuaded Malcolm to agree. But I wonder if you place the same construction on these facts as I do."

"You're saying they create a strong presumption that Malcolm was Jock's son," said Lawson. "I can't accept that on such flimsy evidence, I'm afraid."

"But you do agree it would make a difference, that and Mr. Blake's evidence, to the disposition of the estate."

"If he chose to take action, yes. It would mean washing a great deal of dirty linen in public."

"Exactly what I was thinking," said Richard cordially.

Lawson smiled at him again. "I believe you're trying to threaten me, Mr. Trenton, in the nicest possible way, of course."

"Not threaten...well, not exactly. But I thought you might see that the very meager provision I'm asking you to make for Malcolm Stonor might be an easy way out for everybody."

"Yes, I take your point. But I can't say anything more than I've done already, Mr. Trenton. If Mr. Blake will write to me, setting out what Jock told him quite clearly, I'll put it before the girls. After that it will be up to them."

"I wonder...would you mind very much if I went to see Mrs. Lawson?"

"I shouldn't mind at all, though I don't think you'll find her very susceptible to your ideas," said Philip frankly. "A lioness defending her young, and you know what happens to people who interfere between mother and cubs."

"Yes, I know. All the same, I'd like to take a chance on it," said Richard, feeling for some reason suddenly more cheerful. Lawson had given him a kinder hearing than he felt he had deserved, and perhaps he might have some luck with Eleanor Lawson after all.

He used the telephone before he left and called Bob Blake. Bob was very willing to set down Jock

Thorold's intentions in writing and was inclined to
be hopeful about the outcome. Richard had some
difficulty in persuading him that nothing at all was
likely to come of the exercise.

Lawson had left him alone while he put through
the call but came back into the room now, saying he
himself had used his clerk's phone to speak to his
wife. "She's at home if you want to go there right
away," he said, "but I've a nasty feeling you're going to get a chilly reception."

"I'll have to risk that," said Richard. "I've got
your address written down somewhere, but could
you tell me the best way of getting there?"

II

BEFORE HE WENT to the Lawsons' house Richard
took the opportunity of looking at the place where
Jock Thorold had lived for the last twenty-five
years of his life. It was very near the heath, and a
mansion would have described it better. After his
daughters were married the old man must have felt
quite lost among its splendors. Or perhaps not.
Richard was getting the impression of a self-reliant
man, not easily to be daunted. But he was telling
himself as he walked away that that was nothing
but time wasted; it hadn't added to his sum of
knowledge at all.

Eleanor and Philip Lawson lived only a few
streets away, a more modest dwelling but still of a
quality that Richard felt would have satisfied the
most fastidious. It was another old house, and the
furnishings of the room to which he was shown
looked surprisingly new—not modern, but in keeping with their surroundings, so perhaps Mrs.
Lawson had called in an interior decorator to give
her some ideas. As soon as she joined him he felt
that he had guessed right about that; he also felt,

with a sinking of his spirits, that he wasn't going to get anywhere at all with her. As Bob Blake had said, she was an extremely good-looking woman, tall and fair, and the dark gray dress she wore—was that a concession to mourning, he wondered?—fitted her and suited her ideally. But she had, as Bob Blake had also said, a severe look, and she eyed Richard as though his presence gave her no pleasure at all.

"My husband says you're from the bank," she remarked, "from their head office. I can't understand why you should be calling on us."

"I had the pleasure of talking to your husband earlier, as no doubt he also told you," said Richard carefully. "I should have begun—" if you had given me time, he added to himself, but fortunately did not speak his thought aloud "—by telling you how very sorry I am to hear of your father's death. It must have been a great blow to you."

"A great shock, completely unexpected. But I don't see how that concerns you. Our account has always been in order."

"Certainly it has. My visit has nothing to do with that," Richard told her. "There's a small matter concerning your father's estate."

"Philip says everyone should make a will," said Eleanor, sounding suddenly more human. "But in this case there's no harm done. He can deal with everything, and I understand there's no doubt at all about the application of the laws of intestacy." She was obviously quoting, and Richard smiled a little, trying to take the sting out of his next words.

"Not in law," he said, "not in the letter of the law at least, but perhaps in the spirit."

"What on earth are you talking about?" She was severe again.

"Your father's protégé, Malcolm Stonor."

"That boy! Is he trying to make some claim on the

estate? I assure you, Mr. Trenton, he has no basis for it.''

"So I understand," said Richard, but couldn't resist adding, ''as things stand at present. But there is the matter of Mr. Thorold's intentions for him, which I should imagine would be more important to you.''

"I shall never forgive my father, never," said Eleanor, who didn't seem to have been listening. "To come home like that, bringing a strange boy with him, a factory hand's brat. I was at the house when they arrived and I don't think I shall ever get over the shock. It was a complete surprise to me.''

"Did Mr. Thorold say anything to you, either then or later, that would explain his taking Stonor in?''

"He said Malcolm had nowhere to go, that he was lonely himself and would like a boy about the house. Such nonsense! We've always been a close family, and he had his grandchildren, who visited him quite regularly.''

"Was that all he said, Mrs. Lawson?''

"I think you're making an insinuation that I don't like, Mr. Trenton," she said coldly.

"The possibility must have occurred to you, surely, that Stonor was...related to you, shall we say?''

"If you mean he's my father's illegitimate son, you may as well say so straight out," said Eleanor. "My husband made the same suggestion at the time, and I told him quite plainly it was ridiculous. A woman like that!''

"A woman who did a pretty good job of bringing up her son," said Richard.

"You forget he's lived with my father for five years and attended the best schools. If you'd heard him when he first arrived—''

"Yes, I've no doubt his accent was a little more pronounced then. All the same—''

"As my father never acknowledged him and never went through adoption proceedings, I understand Malcolm can make no claim on the estate."

"Unless the matter is susceptible to proof."

"Did he put you up to this? Malcolm, I mean. Did he tell you some story—that his mother had told him on her deathbed, for instance? Some such nonsense."

"No, he told me nothing like that. I should explain, Mrs. Lawson, that I'm really asking very little of the estate on his behalf, and that only because it has come to my knowledge what Mr. Thorold's intentions were."

"How could that be?"

"From someone in whom he confided, someone I have every reason to trust." He had mentioned Bob Blake to Philip Lawson, but this lady was a man-eater, and—forgetting for the moment that Lawson had declared his intention of showing Bob's statement to Jock Thorold's daughters—he felt it wouldn't be advisable to betray Eleanor's local bank manager to her. He repeated Blake's story, however, almost in the same words he had used to her husband. "You're quite right in saying Malcolm Stonor has no legal claim," he concluded, "but in the circumstances I thought perhaps the family might feel it was reasonable to continue his allowance until he qualifies as a solicitor. That's quite a modest request, isn't it?"

"In the circumstances I think it an extremely impertinent one," said Eleanor, who obviously wasn't one to mince her words. "Malcolm has no cause for complaint at all; he is considerably better qualified to face the world than he was five years ago. Why did you come to me, Mr. Trenton? Philip must have told you the family's position."

"I'd hoped to be able to persuade you—"

"You thought that, as a member of the weaker

sex, I'd be more susceptible," she interrupted him.

"No, I don't think that was in my mind at all. I got the impression that your husband respected your opinion—" that was a good way of putting it, he thought "—and that, perhaps, the other members of your family would do so, too."

"It has nothing to do with Philip really," she retorted. "Only with myself and my sisters. We're quite unanimous, and I have no intention at all of using my influence, as you call it, to change their minds."

No use pointing out to her that he hadn't actually used those words.

"Very well, then, Mrs. Lawson, I must apologize for troubling you," said Richard, getting to his feet. Afterward it was to occur to him that the interview had left him without a shred of dignity, but for the moment he was conscious only of a rising anger.

"You haven't troubled me in the slightest," she told him. "Once I've made up my mind, that's it. And a very good thing, too. Philip is just as sentimental as you are. I have to be strong for us both."

"Yes, I can see that," said Richard gently. He was on his way to the door when it burst open and a young man came into the room. Richard's first thought was that there was no mistaking the fact that the newcomer was Eleanor's son; there was a strong likeness between them, though no such hardness in his expression.

"Oh, hello!" he said amiably to Richard. "You're the bloke from the bank."

"Mr. Trenton is just leaving," said Eleanor coldly.

"No—but I want to hear what it was all about. You shouldn't have told me he was coming if you didn't want to rouse my curiosity." He paused there, eyeing Mrs. Lawson critically. "You've been giving the poor chap a rough time, ma," he said accusingly.

"How many times have I told you I will not be called by that odious diminutive. Mother is a perfectly good word."

"Darling, don't put on airs with me," he pleaded, and turned to Richard again. "I'm Phil Lawson," he said. "At your service."

"Mr. Trenton is just leaving," said Eleanor Lawson again.

"Well, aren't you going to enlighten me?"

This time his mother was goaded into replying. "Mr. Trenton's visit concerned Malcolm Stonor," she said. "He knows my opinion on the subject and there's no more to be said."

"Yes, but. . . why should the bank be concerning itself with him? Anyway he's a decent enough sort. I like him. And you know what dad thinks."

Richard found his voice. "What does Mr. Lawson think?" he inquired. But he was pretty sure he'd got the family's measure by now.

"Well, that something ought to be done for him," said Phil. "Joanna thinks so, too."

"You may show Mr. Trenton to the door, Phil," said Eleanor Lawson in a tone that didn't invite any argument.

"I'll do more than that," said Phil amiably. "I'll walk to the bus stop with him. Or do you want a taxi?" he added, as they went out into the hall.

"No, the bus stop will do very well. I'm Richard Trenton," he added as they went down the steps to the short drive, "and your mother was quite right: I've no business at all really, no excuse for concerning myself with your family's affairs."

"You're going to tell me it's a matter of simple justice," said Phil. "I know that and so does dad. But try moving mother on the subject, or either of my aunts for that matter. Poor Malcolm, his coming absolutely infuriated them all."

"I can understand that in a way," said Richard. "But I've been wondering—"

"You want to know who Joanna is," said Phil with more perception than Richard would have given him credit for. "She's a bone of contention if you want to know, though I don't think she'd appreciate the phrase herself. Joanna Martin, the girl next door. I've been courting her for a couple of years—see how my plebeian origins will out—as soon as I suddenly noticed she'd grown into quite a beauty from being a leggy little girl. The complication is that Malcolm fell for her, too, and to tell you the truth, I don't know which of us she favors. She's a bit of a flirt, to tell you the truth, but of course she's only nineteen. And shall I tell you something? I shouldn't like her to agree to marry me just because Malcolm didn't have any money."

Richard smiled at that rather ingenuous statement. "I gather that if it was up to you—"

"I'd give the poor chap a good start in life at least. As it is, you know, he might have been happier if old Jock had never brought him south. It can't have been easy for him. Have you ever thought what it would be like going to a decent school with a broad Yorkshire accent? But he fought his way through all that, and now to be left without a penny . . .! I like him," he added unnecessarily.

"Yes, I had gathered that." Richard spoke a little dryly. "I think I ought to tell you that it isn't Malcolm's idea to make any claim on your grandfather's estate, but Mr. Thorold confided his intentions to one of my colleagues, and it is felt we should make an attempt to get them carried out at least in part."

"I see," said Phil rather blankly. "You've seen Malcolm, though?"

"Oh, yes, yesterday. Mr. Fulford is putting him on salary, if you're worried about that, but I gather it won't be much more than the office boy would get. He'll have to be pretty careful.''

"One of us could have given him a home," said Phil, kicking aside a stone that lay in his path. "Well, I wouldn't have liked to ask him to share ours actually, because I think mother would have frozen him out within a week. And Uncle Max and Aunt Geraldine have a whole horde of kids; it's not so bad during termtime but when the holidays come round it must be pretty grim. As for Aunt Alexandra...no, I don't think that would do, either. They've only one daughter, quite a kid, but Uncle Wilf isn't exactly a sympathetic character, except as far as his affection for Ginny is concerned. That's my cousin—her full name is Virginia.''

"My wife and I live in a small block of flats called Eden Place," said Richard. "It's just at the end of Bread Court, where Malcolm works. Maggie is trying to get him a room there on the ground floor; there are some studios for rent and I believe one is vacant. It wouldn't cost very much, and as he pointed out himself he'd save on fares.''

"That's good of you, and something of a relief. I haven't asked you how you got on with this project of yours," he went on, "because it was pretty obvious when I came in that mother was in one of her less amenable moods. You know, Mr. Trenton—or may I call you Richard?—I really meant it when I said that Malcolm might have been happier if he'd been left in Leeds. There's mother, and my two aunts, of course, who were all grown up when they came south. Mother never lets up for a moment with that grande dame attitude of hers; she's afraid people will remember her background. Grandfather Jock didn't always have money, you know.''

"So I understood, but I expect they'd been quite well-off for some time before the move was made.''

"I think so, none of them talk about that time

much. But you didn't know Jock; he was a grand old boy, not a bit of pretentiousness about him at all. He'd never forget an old friend, and I expect as long as they lived in Leeds there was a constant stream of visitors from his earlier, less affluent days. Mother wouldn't like that at all.'' He hesitated, and then added in something of a rush, ''What are you going to do now, Richard?''

That brought a silence. Then, ''Talk to my wife,'' said Richard. ''I think that's the first thing.''

''Are you going to give up without any further struggle?''

''What do you think I can do?''

Phil grinned at him. ''Prove that Malcolm is my uncle,'' he said. ''Come now, that must have occurred to you. We were good friends, you know, in spite of my being three years older. He told me quite a bit about his life with his mother, and I'm a lawyer, too. I know quite well it would make all the difference.''

''It had occurred to me,'' admitted Richard, rather reluctantly.

''And now,'' said Phil, with one of his flashes of insight, ''you're so absolutely furious with mother, you think you'd like to prove that just to spite her.''

''Something like that,'' Richard conceded, rather startled.

''Well, if it's any comfort to you, go ahead with my blessing,'' said Phil.

''Thank you. Would you say the same thing, Phil, if I told you it might mean his being awarded a considerable bite out of the estate?''

''I'd say exactly the same thing. It's easy for me, because I've never wanted for anything, and I daresay dad will see to it that I never do. But here's the bus stop, and here's your bus,'' he added, looking along the road. ''I'll be in touch with Malcolm, of

course, but I'd be obliged if you'd let me know how
you get on."

"I will," Richard promised, and swung himself
onto the bus. Phil Lawson, amiable to the last,
raised his hand in farewell before he turned away.

III

Richard lunched with Jake as he had promised,
and when the solicitor asked him, as Phil Lawson
had done, what he was going to do next, he gave
him the same reply. If Fulford didn't see what value
Maggie Trenton's opinion would have, he didn't say
so, but remarked instead, "All that you've told me
is more or less what I expected."

"Yes, but it had to be done," said Richard. "At
least Malcolm has a good friend in Lawson's son."

"Yes, he's mentioned him to me. I'd be glad, to
tell you the truth, to hear that Phil had got in touch
with him, because I think Malcolm feels that the
family has completely cast him off."

"Besides," said Richard, "there's this girl."

"Yes, you mentioned her. Joanna Martin, was it?
But what about her?"

"I don't imagine Malcolm would feel able to approach her again in his present circumstances."

"What has that got to do with Phil getting in
touch with him?"

"I think he's generous minded enough to bring
them together again. Or it may be only for his own
sake. He doesn't want to win her by default."

"That's too high-minded for me," said Jake
frankly. "Are you going back to work this afternoon?"

"Not on your life. If Jarvis wants his dirty work
done for him he's got to pay for it in my time. I'm
just going into the branch at head office to ask
about the finances of Lawson's firm, as that's

where they keep their account. But after that," he added firmly, "I'm going home."

The errand didn't take him very long, so it transpired that he got home before Ricky, and Maggie was pleased to see him, though not, in all the circumstances, surprised. "We've time to have tea in peace before the offspring comes in," she said, rather pleased by the prospect, though Richard knew well enough that she was secretly dreading, as he was himself, the day that Ricky would be old enough for boarding school. "So you can tell me all about everything while we drink it." She was speaking casually, carefully not expressing her extreme curiosity, but Richard was in no doubt that she was interested, especially when she set down the tray of tea things and stretched herself luxuriously. That was to show him that she was in a receptive mood, but he was also in no doubt that there was a little worry underlying the interest.

So he went over yet again his talk with Philip Lawson, with Eleanor, and then with Phil. "And after lunch I went up to head office," he finished, "to inquire into Lawson's finances—as a firm, I mean. The firm's account is with our city branch, and the clients' account, and they're both extremely healthy. There has never been any question of borrowing, which is a pity in its way, because he seems to me just the sort of chap it would be a pleasure to do business with."

"All the same," said Maggie, her eyes on his face, "you're angry, Richard, darling. I am right, aren't I?"

"Right enough," Richard admitted. It was a thing that didn't often happen, and he'd been trying to disguise the feeling from himself for several hours.

"Could you tell me exactly why?" Maggie put the question a little diffidently. "I can understand your being disappointed at not being able to do what you set out to accomplish, but that's not all it is, is it?''

"Eleanor Lawson got under my skin," Richard confessed. "You ought to have heard her, Maggie. She was so damned superior, talking about a factory worker's brat—she meant Malcolm—when, after all, her own father was self-made, and not a bit ashamed of it as far as I can tell. It made me feel I was going to do something about young Stonor no matter how much opposition there was from the family. And the only way I can see of helping him is to try to prove that Jock Thorold really was his father, but I want your agreement before I go ahead.''

For a moment Maggie ignored that last remark. "I know you told me the law is a lot more—more understanding than it used to be where illegitimate children are concerned," she said, "but how could you set about doing that?''

"The only thing I can think of is to go to Leeds and make a few inquiries. Lilian Stonor must have had some friends; perhaps I can find out something from them.''

"But you said...didn't you say Malcolm would have to take some action to get himself included in the settlement of the estate?''

"Yes, I think that's true.''

"But you also said he wouldn't be willing to.''

"I'm quite sure he wouldn't. His attitude is that old Jock did pretty well by him, and he has no claim on the family. I think he's absolutely genuine about that.''

"Well, then!" said Maggie, and left it at that.

"Even without his doing anything the position would be changed," Richard explained. "If they knew it could be proved that he was a blood relative it might change their attitude altogether. Somebody used the phrase 'dirty linen,' which is rather trite but tremendously apt in the circumstances. Nobody wants theirs washed in public.''

"You mean you would go to them and threaten them? That doesn't sound like you, Richard.''

"I think threat is too strong a word. I will admit that Jake says it sounds perilously like blackmail, though in fairness to myself I should add that the idea seemed to amuse him, but I don't see it that way. I could gently point out the position and leave it at that.''

"You really are angry,'' said Maggie, half-admiringly. "Why do you say it's up to me whether you go on with this?''

"Because, my dearest dear, I had my instructions from Jarvis, and I'll be exceeding them by about two thousand miles. It's nothing to do with him how I occupy my spare time, but I can't help feeling he'll take it amiss.''

"Yes, that's what I've been afraid of. All the same, Richard, you can't let it stop you. I quite see you've got to do what you feel is right.''

"Even though I only think it's right because I've lost my temper?'' said Richard in a teasing tone, but she answered quite seriously.

"Yes, even in that case. Does that mean you're going to make these inquiries in Leeds over the weekend?''

"Yes, I thought I'd take the train this evening and come back tomorrow night if at all possible. It's more likely to be Sunday, though.''

"Well, that can't be helped.'' Maggie was doing her best to sound philosophical, though actually she hated his being away. "Ricky is going to wonder, though. You know he's already got it into his head that you're engaged in police business again.''

"Yes, I do know it for my sins,'' said Richard ruefully. "Can you cope, do you think?''

"Oh, yes, I can cope.'' They heard the front door then, and the clatter in the hall that heralded

Ricky's arrival. "But you can explain to him that you're going away, Richard," said Maggie firmly, "while I telephone the station and pack an overnight bag for you."

"All right," said Richard, not too enthusiastically, and set himself, as his son burst into the room, to face the barrage of questions that was bound to follow.

5

RICHARD WENT NORTH on an intercity train and whiled away the journey by dining, surprised to find—for he did not often leave London—that eating at a hundred and twenty-five miles an hour was quite easy and that the half bottle of wine he allowed himself showed no tendency to slop out of the glass. He spent the night at the Queen's Hotel, which had the added advantage of being convenient to the station, and set out early the next morning to the address that Malcolm Stonor had given him. He had the name of the friend who had looked after Malcolm in his younger years; she had still been in residence in Pleasant Street at the time of Lilian Stonor's death, but after a further five years he was rather doubtful of finding her. However, he was quite prepared to knock on a few doors in the hopes of tracing some of her former fellow workers, and when the taxi driver deposited him outside one of the row of terrace houses his hopes in that direction began to soar. They were in the very shadow of the factory, and the name Tam O'Shanter glared at him from a rather vividly painted sign across the road.

The taxi driver, who had accepted his original instructions without comment, looked around him disparagingly as Richard felt in his pocket for his fare. "Want me to wait for you?" he inquired. "You'll never find another cab out here."

"Not even if I walk back to the main road that we just turned off?" asked Richard.

"Not a chance."

"The trouble is, you see, I may be some time. Do you mind waiting?"

The driver glanced at his watch. "Give you until eleven o'clock for a fiver," he offered. But he added, with some belated impulse of honesty, "There's a station here, you know. You could get a train that would take you right back to town."

"Yes, but how often do the trains run?" And how many stop in a godforsaken place like this, he might have added. But the question was rhetorical; he didn't wait for a reply. "I'd like to take you up on your offer," he said, "if you're sure you won't be losing by it."

"Tell you the truth, not much trade at this time of year," said the driver confidingly. "Give me time to read the morning paper, too."

"All right, then." Richard turned away and surveyed the door in front of him, a green door, newly painted. Now that he came to look more closely, he saw that, though the taxi driver had despised the address he had been given, there was an air of self-respect about the street that he ought to have anticipated from Malcolm's description but that he had failed to take into account.

There was a brass knocker on the door—a woman three doors down was polishing hers and looked at him curiously—and he made use of it, not too roughly. There was no immediate reply, however, and the woman down the street called out to him, "Try a little harder. She's a bit deaf and sometimes she doesn't hear." Richard thanked her, and thus encouraged plied the knocker again.

This time the door was opened almost immediately by a pleasant-looking woman of about fifty in a neat print frock. "Well?" she said, rather more sharply than he would have expected from her appearance. "What do you want, young man?"

"I'm looking for Mrs. Margaret Welford. I wonder—" Richard began, but wasn't allowed to finish.

"Then you've come to the right place, haven't you?" she inquired, looking him up and down. Richard sustained her scrutiny in silence for a moment, and she was obviously satisfied by what she saw. "Now, then, no use standing on the doorstep," she told him. "You'd best come in." Neither then nor later did he notice any sign of the hardness of hearing her neighbor had mentioned. Thinking it over, he decided she must be an expert at lipreading.

Richard thanked her and followed her across the threshold, carefully stepping over its whitened surface. They were immediately in what she would undoubtedly have called the parlor, but he was relieved to see that there were distinct signs that it was lived in. A newspaper on the floor, several paperbacks lying about and a cup of tea almost full on a table near one of the easy chairs. "I'm afraid I'm interrupting you," Richard said. It wasn't the first time the awkwardness of his quest had struck him, but it was brought home to him very forcibly now.

"Just having me elevenses," said Mrs. Welford, making Richard wonder at what unearthly hour she rose if something just past nine could be regarded as the middle of the morning. "Want a cuppa?"

"That would be very nice." He could have well done without it, but she seemed to have accepted him and he didn't want to do anything to disturb that desirable state of affairs.

"Only be a jiffy." She was true to her word and back almost immediately with another cup, already with milk in it and two lumps of sugar in the saucer.

"Now, then," she said, seating herself. "Sit down and be comfortable and tell me what you want."

"Do you remember the Stonors?" asked Richard tentatively.

"Lilian and Malcolm. Of course I do. Lived next to me for sixteen years, didn't she, and the boy almost as long? I used to baby-sit him, you know, a grand lad he was." And then, with belated caution, "Why are you asking about them?"

"It's a matter of inheritance," said Richard, which sounded impressive and had the advantage of being true.

"You're one of these lawyers, then?"

"No, a banker as a matter of fact. My name's Trenton, Richard Trenton."

"Comes to the same thing," she said airily. "I can give you Malcolm's address if that's what you want. Sends me a Christmas card every year, he does, and promises one of these days to come and see me. He's doing what they call his articles, you know, going to be a solicitor himself. Well, he says there's a lot of studying to be done, but when he gets through all his exams he'll be paying me a visit."

"That's kind of you, Mrs. Welford, but it isn't his address I need. I saw him only two days ago and I know the senior partner of the firm he's articled with. But Mr. Jock Thorold has died, and the question of Malcolm's parentage has become rather important. I can't explain any further to you. I hope you'll forgive me for that, but it's extremely confidential."

"Know how to hold your tongue, do you? I like that in a man. But I can't help you, lad, I just don't know."

"Perhaps if you'd start from the beginning, from your first acquaintance with Mrs. Stonor, something might emerge that would be helpful."

"You're really on Malcolm's side?"

"I certainly am," said Richard firmly, and again had to undergo that close scrutiny. Again apparently he passed the test with flying colors.

"All right, then." She picked up her cup of tea and drank with relish. "Drink that while it's hot," she commanded. "T'pot's on t'stove and I can get you another one in a trice."

"Thank you," said Richard meekly, and also picked up his cup. He didn't like milk in his tea, but this was no time to say so. "How long have you lived here, Mrs. Welford?"

"Me? Oh, twenty-five years or more. It's convenient, you know. I work across the road at t'factory—at least I do since my husband died."

"I'm sorry to hear that," said Richard.

"Oh, twenty-three years ago," said Mrs. Welford cheerfully. "Got into an argument with a tram when he'd had a drop too much, that was the trouble. Well, we had no kids so I got myself a job, and all things considered it's done well by me all these years. Jock was a good employer, you know, and wasn't above seeing to things himself when he came north, even after he went all la-di-da living in London. You'll not think me forward calling him Jock, everybody does."

"Yes, I've gathered that already. I wish I'd known him," said Richard sincerely. "I think he sounds a grand old boy."

"That's true enough," she said consideringly. "Anyway, you're not interested in me. Lilian came here twenty years ago, just before the boy was born. Called herself Mrs. Stonor, which I think was natural, but we got to be good friends and she told me later it was just a tale. There wasn't any Mr. Stonor and never had been."

"She confided so much to you, but didn't tell you who Malcolm's father was?"

"No, she never mentioned that."

"I understand from Malcolm that she'd sometimes be away from home for a few days at a time, and that when he was quite small he used to stay with you on these occasions."

"That's true enough. I was glad to have him, he was no bother at all. Mind you, by the time he was eight he was a self-reliant kid. Lilian used to leave him plenty of food and know he'd be all right. But I'm not saying he didn't spend a good deal of time with me even then. We were always good friends."

"What I'm wondering, you see," said Richard tentatively, "is where Mrs. Stonor went."

"Well, I'll tell you one thing, young man," said Mrs. Welford, suddenly fierce again, "she was a respectable woman for all the boy can't say who his father was."

"Yes, I'm sure of it. I think you're trying to tell me, Mrs. Welford, that she might have been seeing one man all that time—Malcolm's father perhaps—but that there was no question of her being promiscuous."

"I suppose that word will do as well as any other," she said grudgingly. "Yes, that was near enough what I meant, young man."

"Do you remember her last illness?"

"Now, is that a thing I could forget? She was ill the whole winter, you know, and only in St. James's the last few days, when the end was near. It was hard on Malcolm."

"I wouldn't wonder if it was hard on you, too, Mrs. Welford," said Richard. "You had your own work, but I expect you spent a good deal of time with her."

"That's right, and I saw t'lad had enough to eat. There were other people as helped, too. They're friendly, you know, round here."

"And she had another visitor?"

"You may as well say straight out what you
mean. You mean Jock Thorold, don't you?"

"He was in my mind," Richard agreed.

"Well, he came whenever he was visiting the factory. She was an old employee, you must realize
that. He'd have done the same for any of us."

"I'm quite willing to take your word for that, but
if the employee had been somebody else, would he
have more or less adopted her son?"

"Didn't he adopt him, then? I understood he was
going to."

"He had to go to the local authorities to arrange
guardianship, I understand. Perhaps that's what
gave you the idea."

"No, I know all about that. A lot of fuss about
nothing. But he told me quite definitely that if
things worked out he would be adopting the boy as
his own."

"Mrs. Welford, did he tell you anything else?"

"Now what would you be meaning by that?" she
asked suspiciously.

Nothing for it but to be blunt. "I'm sure the
possibility has occurred to you that Malcolm was his
natural son."

"I don't know nowt about that."

"But hasn't the idea crossed your mind?" he insisted.

"Old Jock didn't say anything to me, and neither
did Lilian." She gazed at Richard in silence for
a long moment. "Well, then, I may as well tell
you," she said at last. "I always thought it was
him she was going to when she took off. Why else
would it always have been just when he was in
town?"

Richard suppressed a sudden stab of excitement.
"Did you know Lilian before she came to live in this
street?" he asked.

"Not well. Only to see her in the factory, and

perhaps exchange a word when we went to the counting house to get our pay.''

"So you know nothing of her life at the time Malcolm was conceived.''

"Not a thing.''

"Not even where she lived, who her parents were?''

"No, I'd say she was a bit closemouthed and I am not nosy. But one thing I can tell you, Stonor was her maiden name. That's what she used at the factory anyway. It was only when she came here to have the boy that she started using Mrs.''

"I see. You don't have any idea where she went on those occasions?''

"No idea in the world. And if you want my guess, Mr. Trenton, it would be nowhere in Leeds. Jock was well-known here. Some village not too far away, I wouldn't wonder.''

One thing was certain; he couldn't undertake that kind of detective work. "Malcolm said they never wanted for anything,'' he remarked. "Do you know how she lived during the period of her pregnancy, for instance, and again during her last illness?''

"She had her benefits, you know, but I always thought. . . well, since I've been frank with you I may as well say it right out. I thought Jock was helping her. She was a whole year away from work when Malcolm was born and never seemed to have any difficulty paying for someone to look after him after that.''

"If Jock Thorold had been Malcolm's father,'' said Richard thinking it out, "I'd have expected him to set her up somewhere, not let her go back to work in the factory.''

"You're saying that because you didn't know Lilian,'' said Margaret Welford positively. "Independent she was, and I admire her for it. Not but what she wouldn't think it fair to get a bit of help on the side.''

All cash transactions no doubt, and not a hope of tracing them. ''Did Mrs. Stonor have a bank account by any chance?'' asked Richard, not too hopefully.

''Bank account? What would she want with a thing like that? No, of course she didn't.''

''The person who looked after Malcolm when both you and his mother were at work—can you put me in touch with her?''

'' 'Fraid not. She died two years back.''

''Any other of Lilian's friends, then. Was there anyone she was particularly close to?''

''No one as close as me,'' said Mrs. Welford positively, and he could well believe her. ''There's two as live in this street and I'll write their names and numbers down for you, if that's what you want, but you'll find they can't be as much help as I've been.''

''No, and I'm very grateful to you. There's just one more thing...the chief cashier at Tam O'Shanter, is it the same man as it was in Mrs. Stonor's time?''

''Aye, it is. Ted Gill, getting on to retirement he is now.'' She came to her feet and made her way to an old-fashioned bureau at the side of the room. ''Shall I add him to the list?''

''If you please.'' He waited until she had finished writing and handed him a sheet of paper, and then thanked her again and started toward the door.

''Just a minute, lad,'' she stopped him. ''Has any of what I've told you done young Malcolm any good?''

''That's a difficult question to answer, Mrs. Welford. It isn't proof—''

''You mean,'' she said, furrowing her brow, ''that if we could prove he was Jock's son it would help him?''

No harm in admitting as much as that. "I think it would," said Richard.

"I don't understand these legal things," said Mrs. Welford, sounding as if she was just as glad that she didn't. "You've taken this to heart, haven't you, young man?" she added with more perception than he would have expected of her. "Do your best for him, I wouldn't wonder."

"I shall try to," Richard promised her. "And I shall remember your kindness." After that he made his escape before she could offer him another cup of milky tea.

II

"BUT SHE WAS RIGHT about the other two women not being able to help me," he told Maggie that evening. It had been late when he got home, long after Ricky's bedtime, and they were sitting companionably together over a nightcap. "There'd been some talk when Thorold took Malcolm away with him; that was only to be expected. But I know what Jake Fulford will say when I tell him; it's nothing like proof."

"He must be Malcolm's father," said Maggie. "Jock Thorold, I mean. There's absolutely no other explanation of all Mrs. Welford told you."

"I think that, too. I only hope I can use the presumption to persuade the family that something ought to be done."

"Does that mean you'll be busy all day tomorrow?" said Maggie suspiciously.

"Yes, I'm afraid it does. Was Ricky a dreadful nuisance today?"

"No more than usual," said his fond mother. "The picture is finished."

"The child and the mother and the flea?" said

Richard, grinning. "I thought it was finished already."

"Yes, that one. I know he said he was finished, but then he thought of a few improvements. So I took him to the zoo, and he spent the evening trying to draw the bears from memory. Actually, they weren't too bad. I think he's better at sketching than he is at painting."

"What did you tell him about my absence?"

"Business," said Maggie. "The trouble is, he's heard that before when it hasn't been exactly true. Anyway, I'll think of something to keep him amused tomorrow, but you haven't told me about this Mr. Gill, the cashier. You said Mrs. Welford gave you his address."

"Yes, and that's really the only reason why I'm so late home. I think Lilian must have been a favorite of his. Anyway, he was willing enough to take my word for it that my questions would help her son, and not ask any of his own. We spent the whole afternoon in the counting house—yes, they actually still have a counting house—going over all the old ledgers to see if we could find any special payments that had been made to Mrs. Stonor, particularly around the time of Malcolm's birth, and then again during her last illness. But there was nothing, nothing at all. It was exactly as I expected: Jock must have done the whole thing in cash. Malcolm just took it for granted that the money came from the factory."

"I suppose you couldn't pretend—" said Maggie, and broke off laughing when she saw the horrified expression in her husband's eyes.

"No, I could not!" he said very firmly. "If I could get away with it with the Fieldings and the Bennetts, remember Philip Lawson is a lawyer, and the first thing he'd do would be to ask for proof."

"I suppose you're right," said Maggie resignedly. "What are your plans for tomorrow?"

"I have to do some phoning first. I'd like to see the other two families, particularly the two younger daughters. Then I suppose I might try Lawson again. I liked him, you know; left to himself he'd do the right thing. But he's no match for his wife."

"I've never known you to take such dislike to anybody," said Maggie. "It isn't like you, Richard, darling."

"Like me or not, that's how I feel, and so would you if you'd met her." But he felt that as much had been said about the subject as could be useful, and took the opportunity of Maggie suddenly yawning cavernously to suggest that they seek their bed.

6

OVERNIGHT RICHARD THOUGHT BETTER of his plans, which meant, Maggie said accusingly when he told her about it over breakfast, that he must have been lying awake for hours. "I didn't sleep very well," he admitted. "I don't think you can wonder at that. Though you must admit this new idea is better than the one I was proposing when I talked to you last night."

"That you should phone Philip Lawson and try to arrange to see the whole family at his house," said Maggie thoughtfully. Ricky seemed very well occupied in extracting the bones from a kipper, but they were watching their words all the same. The boy looked up now.

"I thought if you did get home last night, daddy, we could go on top of the bus to Hampton Court today. The weather is perfectly scrumptious, and you know when Hugh and Jane come home for the holidays it's bound to start raining."

"I'm afraid you're right about that, but I can't oblige you today," his father told him. "It's a good idea, though. I don't see why we couldn't do it next weekend."

"Promise?" Ricky insisted.

"If at all possible," said Richard cautiously. "You know things crop up sometimes that I can't get out of."

"Yes, I know," said Ricky, sighing. "Who are this

family anyway that you and mummy are talking about?''

"Some customers of the bank," said Richard truthfully.

"In that case you should arrange to see them during business hours," said Ricky in a very superior sort of way. "Unless. . .is there something special going on, daddy? Will that Chief Inspector Denby be coming here again?"

"You asked me that before," said Richard, "and the answer is still the same. Heaven forbid."

"Well, I think it's very interesting," said Ricky. "Much more interesting than all that dull stuff about making people loans." He looked down at his plate where the food was beginning to look distinctly the worse for wear, and sighed again. "If you won't tell me about it I suppose you won't," he said pathetically.

"You're quite right, old son, I won't," said Richard. "But you're all wrong, you know."

"Then I suppose these people, this family of Mr. Lawson's that you're talking about, want to borrow millions and millions of pounds," said Ricky dreamily. "That might be almost as exciting as helping the police. It's the dreary little sums of money that I object to."

"Those dreary little sums form our bread and butter," said Richard, who hadn't yet quite despaired of someday getting that fact over to his son. "And this isn't anything to do with a loan," he added incautiously, prompted in all probability by some innate sense of fair play.

"Well, then—"

"Eat your kipper, Ricky, darling," said Maggie, feeling it was time to intervene. "Your father has to telephone, and we'd better think what we're going to do with the day. I think Hampton Court should be an expedition for the three of us, because daddy knows so much more of its history. But we might go to the park and see what boats are being sailed on the Serpentine.''

While Ricky was considering this question, Richard made his escape to the little room he called his study. It was a dreary little place, but at least keeping the telephone on the desk there enabled him to have some privacy when this was necessary. He thought it was Phil Lawson's voice that answered the phone, but he didn't identify himself. Just asked for Mr. Philip Lawson.

''Yes, he's here. Who shall I...I know your voice,'' said the man at the other end. ''You were here on Friday, weren't you, to see my mother?''

''That's right. I'd seen your father before that, though I don't know if that was mentioned when you were present.''

''And now you want to talk to him again, Richard,'' said Phil thoughtfully. ''Well, I don't see why you shouldn't. I'll go and fetch him.''

Philip Lawson sounded definitely cautious when he came to the telephone, so that Richard wondered whether his wife was within earshot. ''Trenton?'' he asked. ''I thought we'd concluded our business together.''

''I had the pleasure of meeting your wife after I left you,'' said Richard mendaciously. The meeting had indeed taken place, but there had been no pleasure about it at all.

''Yes, you told me you were going to see her, and *she* told me about your visit,'' said Philip, sounding a little more sure of himself now. ''As far as I'm concerned the matter is closed; there's nothing more to discuss.''

''I'm sorry to seem insistent, but I think there is,'' said Richard. ''I spent yesterday in Leeds—went up on Friday night as a matter of fact.''

That brought a dead silence at the other end of the line for what seemed like several minutes. "I can't imagine what you thought you could do there," said Lawson at last.

"I talked to a number of people, to a Mrs. Margaret Welford in particular," said Richard, as casually as he could. "Has Malcolm ever mentioned her to you?"

"Not that I remember."

"What she had to tell me was . . . illuminating," said Richard hoping he sounded enigmatic, though he didn't feel that was really his style. "I should like to talk the matter over with all Mr. Thorold's daughters, Mrs. Fielding and Mrs. Bennett as well as Mrs. Lawson."

Another silence. "You don't need my permission to talk to them," said Lawson harshly.

"I'm aware of that. What I'm suggesting is that it might be convenient to see the whole family together if you could arrange that. I should be more obliged to you than I can say."

"Would you indeed?" Philip's tone was definitely skeptical. "You want to meet the family en masse, presumably here," he went on. "We're a formidable bunch all together, and so I warn you."

"I realize I'd be putting myself much in the position of Daniel entering the lions' den," said Richard, and wondered immediately whether that was a tactful way of putting it. To his relief Lawson laughed, and sounded genuinely amused.

"And what if I refuse?" he asked.

"I shall talk the matter over with Mr. Fulford tomorrow morning, and consider what action may be taken," said Richard. That was dangerous ground, and he knew perfectly well there was nothing to be done with the information at his disposal, but he was still angry enough to be incautious. A very dangerous state of mind for a banker, as he knew well enough, but fortunately this was Sunday.

. Again Philip Lawson seemed to be considering. "Very well," he said finally. "Will you give me your number and I'll ring you back when I have spoken to them? If I can arrange a meeting for today, I will. But I ought to warn you that I don't think my wife will be pleased to see you, and from the reaction when she briefed her sisters on your activities I don't think they will be particularly favorably disposed, either."

"I'm prepared for that," said Richard. "I'll wait for your call, then."

The return call came a mere twenty minutes later, which made Richard feel for a moment that his indiscretion had been justified. "If you haven't thought better of your rashness," said Lawson, and again there was a note of amusement in his voice, "the whole family will be assembled here by the time you can arrive. My son, Phil, wants to sit in on the meeting. I take it you've no objection to that."

"No objection in the world," said Richard sincerely. He thought he might well have occasion to feel grateful for having a friend at court.

And he had to admit when he arrived at Hampstead that the family, seen all together, was a little overwhelming. Phil Lawson let him in and put his finger to his lips when Richard was about to speak. "Don't say a word," he advised in a low voice. "I'm on your side, but I ought to warn you that the rest of them are mad as fire. Except dad, of course, but he won't say a word with mother there."

"That's much what your father told me," said Richard, also pitching his voice low. "Shall we get it over with?"

Phil gave him quite a brilliant smile. "You're a determined cuss, aren't you?" he said. "But your blood is on your own head, you know." He then led the way toward the drawing-room door.

Philip Lawson got up and came across the room to meet them, but the rest of them stayed where they were and eyed Richard stonily. "Phil tells me you've met before," said Lawson, obviously assuming an ease he did not feel. "And you've met my wife, I know." Richard murmured something and received the merest inclination of the head from Eleanor Lawson. "This is her sister, Geraldine Fielding, and her husband, Maxwell. And Jock's youngest daughter, Alexandra, and her husband, Wilfred Bennett. Mr. Richard Trenton, whom the bank sent to see me."

As nobody showed any sign of acknowledging this introduction, Richard felt he might as well take a moment or two to sort out the new faces and to remind himself of what he knew about them. Maxwell Fielding, he had been told, was an architect, a very thin-looking man with a straggle of dark hair across what by rights should have been a bald pate. His wife, Geraldine, was like a bad copy of her sister Eleanor with all her edges blurred, thought Richard to himself. But even in her case there was no denying her good looks. The couple had four children, he remembered, and was only too glad that none of them were present. There was enough sorting out to do as it was.

Turning a little he was able to see the Bennetts, sitting side by side on the sofa near the window. The fact that it was a long sofa and that they were both sitting crowded up at one end of it gave the impression that Alexandra was in her husband's custody. She also had the family's good looks—he wondered whether they came from Jock Thorold or from his wife—but there was no arrogance about her, she had a meek look. Her husband, Wilfred—a builder and contractor, hadn't Bob Blake said, who

worked hand in glove with his brother-in-law?—
was stout and not very tall, but an aggressive type if
ever there was one. It was he who spoke first,
rather to Richard's relief; he hadn't fancied breaking that unfriendly silence. "So this is the man," he
said. "What do you think you're doing, hounding us
like this? Just because we all happen to bank with
the Northumberland and Wessex doesn't give them
a right to dictate our actions. I couldn't believe my
ears when Alex told me—" He broke off there,
probably because he had run out of breath and for
no other reason.

"I should explain," said Richard, "that everything I've done since I left Mr. Lawson's office has
been on my own authority and has nothing to do
with the bank. My mission was merely to put certain facts in front of him as administrator of Mr.
Thorold's estate, and nothing beyond that."

"And he came to see me," said Eleanor, "thinking he'd find me a softhearted fool. And since
then," she added, "heaven knows what he's been
up to."

"As I told your husband, Mrs. Lawson, I've been
up to Leeds," said Richard. If anything had been
needed to stiffen his resolution it was her presence.
He recognized that she had the worst effect on him,
but wasn't in the mood to moderate his remarks
because of that. "It was what I was told there that
made me ask for this meeting."

"And what were you told?"

"Perhaps before I go into that you'd allow me to
make my request once again. I quite understand
that you might not have felt able to grant it on your
own authority, but now you're all here together, all
the people concerned, and you may think better of
that refusal."

"It's a question of the law," said Eleanor. "Isn't
that so, Philip?"

"As matters stand, yes," said Lawson uncomfortably. "However, I gather from what Mr. Trenton said—"

"Yes, I'll come to that in a moment," said Richard hastily. "Mrs. Fielding, may I ask you, do you agree with your sister?"

Geraldine glared at him, creating the illusion for the moment that it was Eleanor who was about to speak. "I was absolutely appalled at what I heard of your insinuations," she said. "That boy has no claim on us, no claim on my father. And to suggest that he should be in some way related to us—"

"That he should be Grandfather Jock's bastard, aunt," said Phil helpfully.

"Be quiet, Phil!" Wilfred Bennett snapped. "Don't take any notice of him, Gerry, we all know it's a lie."

"Can a very tentative suggestion be a lie?" Richard wondered. Nobody answered him directly, but Alexandra Bennett spoke up timidly.

"If it's true, Gerry," she said, "surely we owe Malcolm something."

"You don't know what you're talking about, Alex," said her husband bluntly.

"Just a minute," Richard interrupted. "You feel there might be some truth in that suggestion, Mrs. Bennett?"

"No, I—" She glanced rather fearfully at her husband. "I'm sure you're right, dear," she said. "Father would never have done a thing like that."

"You haven't expressed an opinion, Mr. Fielding," said Richard, turning to the one man who had not so far spoken. "Are you, too, against this small provision being made for Malcolm Stonor?"

"It isn't up to me to have an opinion about it." The architect's voice was rather high-pitched, just the sort of voice you'd expect from a chap who looked like that, Richard thought. "But I agree with my wife, of course; there are the children to consider."

"A simple matter of justice," said Geraldine firmly. "And of not allowing a good man's name to be slandered."

"If it's the children you're thinking of," said Alexandra, unexpectedly waspish, "you've more cause to worry than any of us. Four is rather a big family."

"Just because Wilfred—" began Geraldine hotly, and broke off looking embarrassed. "There isn't any more to be said on the subject. I said before and I say it again, it's a matter of simple justice."

"I gather, however," said Philip Lawson into the silence that followed, "that Mr. Trenton has something to tell us of his activities since Friday."

"Yes, indeed," said Wilfred belligerently. "We should like to hear what you have to say."

Richard took his time looking around the assembled company. "All right, then, I'll tell you," he said, and launched into an account of his talk with Mrs. Margaret Welford, not mincing his words. "I don't think any of you can be in any doubt after that," he said finally, "that Malcolm is really your father's natural son."

"Is what he's told us proof, Philip?" said Maxwell Fielding, looking across at his brother-in-law.

"Not proof, no. But I have to say," he added—and it was odd to hear so self-assured a man sounding almost defiant—"that I agree with Mr. Trenton that it creates a very strong presumption. I shouldn't like to hear the matter aired in court."

"How are we to know that he's telling the truth?" said Bennett, at his most belligerent. "It sounds like a cock-and-bull story to me."

"It could be easily checked," said Richard, hanging on to his temper with both hands.

"The question is," said Eleanor Lawson, "what does Malcolm propose to do about it?"

"I haven't told him yet. And if you want my opinion, Mrs. Lawson, it's what he already believes. I don't think he would have come to live in Hampstead in the first place if he hadn't thought that what I'm now suggesting was true. Mrs. Welford told me that Lilian Stonor was a very independent woman, and I think her son inherited that trait."

"And when you do tell him?" she insisted.

"I think," said Richard, thus driven into a corner, "that he will absolutely decline to take any action at all. He seems to have had nothing but affection from Mr. Thorold, and to bear no resentment to any of you for what I think might be characterized as a rather hostile attitude."

"Very well, then!"

"I did think, however, that what I've told you might make you reconsider your decision. To continue his allowance from the estate wouldn't hurt any of you. What do you say, Mrs. Lawson?"

"I think it a great impertinence that you should even make the suggestion," said Eleanor. "You admit yourself the boy has no claim on us."

Richard let his eyes wander slowly from Geraldine Fielding to Alexandra Bennett. Alexandra glanced at her husband nervously and then shook her head; as for Geraldine's expression, he couldn't read it at all, but her husband might not have been there at all for all the notice she took of his presence. He turned back to the solicitor. "Mr. Lawson?" he said, not very hopefully.

"I'm sure you understand the situation well enough, Mr. Trenton, to know that I must be bound by my wife's and my two sisters-in-law's feelings. They, after all, are the beneficiaries."

Eleanor gave him an impatient look. "There is no need to do anything!" she said trenchantly.

Again when he left, Phil showed Richard off the premises. "I'd walk with you again," he offered, "but I have a sort of feeling I'd like to hear what they're saying in there." He jerked his head toward the drawing-room door as he spoke.

"Nothing that will help me, I'm afraid," said Richard. "By the way, a studio flat is vacant in our building. It's furnished, so I think Malcolm will be moving in this afternoon."

"That's good news. You've discovered he's an independent sort of chap," said Phil, obviously pleased. "I'll try to get hold of Joanna and take a few bottles of beer round by way of celebration this evening. Eden Place, did you say?"

"Yes, an unlikely name, isn't it? At the end of Bread Court. As far as I remember the empty studio is number five, but if you do ring the wrong bell someone will direct you."

"Is it still in order to wish you luck?"

Richard sighed. "I'm afraid not," he said. "I've come to the end of everything I can do. And considerably exceeded my instructions," he added ruefully.

"Why did you do that, I wonder?" asked Phil, genuinely interested.

"Oh, good heavens, I don't know!" Richard, faced with the prospect of having to admit to a good deed, reacted predictably with impatience. "It seemed the obvious thing at the time," he added vaguely.

"Well, all right. You've done what you could and have nothing to reproach yourself with," Phil told him, managing to make the reassurance completely without condescension. "I'll get back now, and if I learn anything to the point I'll knock on your door tonight as well as on Malcolm's."

"We shall be home, and very pleased to see you," said Richard.

"It might be a good idea at that," said Phil thoughtfully. "Even if there isn't anything to report. Malcolm and Joanna deserve a little time together. I know he's been avoiding her the last week or two."

II

IT WASN'T UNTIL EVENING, after Ricky had gone to bed, that Richard found himself alone with Maggie and able to talk over with her his visit to Hampstead. "So you see," he said, as he finished his account of his talk with Jock Thorold's relatives, "the whole thing was a dismal failure. I might as well never have gone to Leeds at all."

"Have you told Mr. Fulford?" said Maggie.

"Yes, I telephoned him when I got home, before you and Ricky got back from your expedition. He's disappointed, of course, but not surprised. Malcolm was still at his house, so he knows, too, by now. At least he's a self-reliant youngster, and I don't think he'll allow the disappointment to spoil his whole life."

"I've said it before," said Maggie thoughtfully, "but I really can't understand those three women. It isn't as if any of them were in desperate need of the money."

"I've been thinking about that," said Richard. "I should say Eleanor is a real dog-in-the-manger type. Couldn't bear the thought of anything she felt was properly hers going to anyone else. Philip Lawson, her husband, would be willing enough to include Malcolm in the settlement, I think, even to the full extent of Jock Thorold's intentions, but he has no choice but to be bound in this matter by his wife's wishes. I have wondered, though; she may wear the trousers in that family, even in a matter that could properly be decided by both of them."

"I don't like the sound of her at all," said Maggie severely and uncharacteristically. "What about the other two?"

"Geraldine, the second sister, was genuinely shocked by the possibility that her father might have had an extramarital affaire, particularly one that led to her having an illegitimate half brother. I couldn't make my mind up about Maxwell Fielding, her husband. From what I have heard he's very successful in his profession, which isn't an easy one. But he has a rather limp air, and I think he'd be willing to be guided by her, even in a matter where he felt he could properly interfere. As for the youngest daughter, Alexandra, the boot's on the other leg."

"What do you mean by that?"

"I have the feeling she'd be willing to be generous, but in her case it's the husband who insists on her remaining adamant about the settlement." As he finished speaking the bell rang and he looked at Maggie incredulously. "Who on earth can that be at this time of the night?" he asked.

"There's just one way of finding out," said Maggie, getting up. "I'll go and see."

A moment later she was back in the room, with Phil Lawson and a slim fair-haired girl behind her. "Mr. Lawson says you were expecting him," she told her husband. "And this is Miss Martin."

"Phil and Joanna," said Phil Lawson. "I told you I might drop in, Richard, and I'm sorry if I'm late, but we were both having dinner at home and somehow it went on and on. And I brought Joanna with me, because Malcolm isn't at home."

"I'm quite sure he said he was moving in this afternoon," said Richard. "In fact, he was packing when I spoke to Jake Fulford on the telephone."

"Yes, that's right. I asked one of the neighbors and they said he'd arrived. But he went out again about nine o'clock. We left the beer on the door-step. Do you think anyone will pinch it?''

"I sincerely hope not. Do sit down, Joanna, and I'll get you a drink. I'm sorry your housewarming party didn't come off.''

"It doesn't matter," said the girl. She had a quiet way of speaking and was, now Richard came to look at her more closely, extremely pretty. "Only neither Phil nor I have seen Malcolm for a while, and we wanted him to know we were on his side. Phil has been telling me everything that's been going on....you needn't worry, Mr. Trenton, I'm absolutely discreet. I won't say anything to anyone about all this.''

Richard, who had probably been looking a little horrified, hastily rearranged his expression. Phil laughed and said, "You can rely on what she says, Richard. She works for my father, and if there's one thing you learn in a solicitor's office it's to keep your mouth shut about other people's affairs. It's the same in the bank, I suppose.''

"Yes," said Richard rather ruefully, "but I think perhaps I haven't been behaving with the utmost discretion myself the last few days." He saw that Maggie had her anxious look, which wasn't at all difficult to arouse, and added hastily, "However, it's all over now as far as I'm concerned, and nothing to worry about. But I do wish I could have helped your friend.''

"I think you've been marvelous," said Joanna, managing to make the compliment sound perfectly genuine. "And if that's cherry brandy I can see on the tray," she added in response to Richard's inquiring look, "that would do splendidly for me. But I think Phil has something to tell you.''

"A change of heart?" said Richard hopefully.

Phil shook his head. "I'm afraid not," he said.

"Oh, never mind, then, I'll get our drinks and

then you can tell me," said Richard. "Cognac, Phil?"

"Thank you." He waited until everyone had been served and then went on. "I'm afraid it isn't anything helpful. Just what was going on when I went back to the drawing room after you left."

"What was going on?" asked Richard, seating himself beside Maggie on the sofa.

"An indignation meeting, I suppose you'd call it," said Phil. "The indignation being mainly on mother's part. Funnily enough, Uncle Wilfred was echoing nearly everything she had to say. It finished up with Aunt Gerry bursting into tears, and having to be taken home by Uncle Max. After that the other two left, as well."

"Mr. and Mrs. Bennett," said Richard to Maggie in explanation. "I had a feeling that Mrs. Bennett wasn't quite so adamant as the others in her opinion."

"No, she wasn't, but Uncle Wilf was," said Phil emphatically. "That was all really."

"Except what happened at dinner tonight," Joanna prompted him.

"Yes, I suppose you might want to hear that, too, as a matter of interest." But he sounded a little less enthusiastic now. "It was just that mother and dad had a knockdown argument over dinner about the matter. You'll have realized that dad is in favor of going at least as far as you asked in the way of helping Malcolm. Anyway, he was absolutely blazingly mad and rushed out of the house before coffee had been served. Which is a thing I've never known him to do before."

"I'm sorry to hear that," said Richard. "I suppose I really was the cause of the dissension as much as Malcolm was."

"I don't think you need blame yourself," said Joanna seriously.

Richard smiled at her. "As long as you don't add that I meant well," he said.

"Do you know what I think?" asked Maggie, entering the conversation suddenly. "I think there's nothing to be done, and we should all forget the matter now, and concentrate—particularly you two—on helping Malcolm to make a new life for himself. You said yourself, Richard, darling, he isn't going to let what's happened ruin everything for him."

"That's right," Richard assented. "But try to remember, Phil, that my research in Leeds led to an indefinite conclusion."

"It's all right, I know the difference between proof and what you call a strong presumption," said Phil. "But I think you're right: we should forget about it. It's odd to think, isn't it," he added pensively, "that it's very likely indeed that Malcolm is really my uncle?"

They stayed half an hour longer, and then left saying that probably Malcolm would be home by now. Maggie was looking at her watch when Richard came back from seeing them out. "Just upon half-past ten," she said. "What a nice young couple. I'm glad that poor young man has got some friends."

"Better than you probably know," Richard told her. "I gather that Phil and Malcolm are rivals for Joanna's hand, but Phil seems afraid of taking advantage of the fact that he can well afford to marry her while Malcolm isn't in such a fortunate position."

"Well, I can understand that," said Maggie. "He wouldn't want to feel she'd accept him for mercenary reasons."

"Somehow, having seen her, I don't think she would," said Richard. "How did she strike you?"

"Just what I said, an awfully nice girl. And really

beautiful, too. A lovely complexion, and I'm quite sure her hair was natural. So very fair, but shining, too.''

"Why is it,'' said Richard sitting down on the sofa again, but this time considerably nearer to his wife, ''that the more beautiful a woman is herself, the more generous she is about another woman's looks?''

7

EVERYTHING SHOULD HAVE BEEN back to normal on Monday morning. Ricky seemed a little disappointed when his father left for the bank as usual. "I daresay you were telling me the truth all along, and it was just business," he said rather grudgingly.

"Ricky, darling, you mustn't say things like that," Maggie protested. "Of course we always tell you the truth."

Ricky's reply to that was a rather skeptical grin. "I shan't go into a bank when I grow up," he said firmly. "I might be a detective myself, or perhaps go into the secret service."

"In either of those occupations," his father told him, "you'll find that jumping to conclusions is neither profitable nor popular with your superiors." But Ricky was irrepressible.

"Come off it, daddy," was all he said.

As a matter of fact, Richard wasn't too sure how he stood with his own superiors that morning, and all through breakfast he'd been concerned to hide his uncertainty from Maggie. Sure enough, at about ten-thirty he was summoned to Edward Jarvis's office. The general manager's attendance on a Monday morning was quite unprecedented, but the invitation came as no surprise to him. "Can't I entrust you with the smallest errand," said Jarvis bitterly by way of greeting, "without your embroiling us in a fight with our customers?"

"I did exactly what you asked me," said Richard defensively, "without any success at all."

"I see. You're about to tell me that what you do on your own time over the weekend is no concern of mine," said Jarvis.

"Something like that," Richard admitted.

"Well, insofar as it concerns the bank, it is very much my affair," Jarvis told him. "Nothing was said about your visiting Mrs. Eleanor Lawson, and you did that on Friday, I understand."

"Yes, and for a very good reason. I thought it might be helpful to the assignment you gave me, because after all, she was one of the persons most concerned."

"And then you went to Leeds?"

"How do you know all this?" asked Richard.

"My own weekend was disturbed by two telephone calls yesterday afternoon," said Jarvis. "One was from Wilfred Bennett, and the other from Mrs. Lawson. I gather Mr. Bennett had obtained my name from his brother-in-law. Mrs. Lawson, however, I met once at a reception."

"Then you know—"

"Nothing that can excuse your conduct."

Richard gave up. "And they told you—"

"They told me exactly what had been said at your interview with the family yesterday."

"I pointed out one or two facts," Richard admitted. "Facts that they might feel were capable of only one interpretation, and that I hoped might change their minds. And if I had succeeded," he added almost belligerently, "you'd be congratulating me on having saved the Tam O'Shanter factory account for one of our branches in Leeds."

"*If* you'd succeeded," said Jarvis meaningfully. "As it is, I don't feel like congratulating you for offending any number of good customers of ours."

"Philip Lawson isn't offended."

"No, but his wife is."

"Then what did they say?" asked Richard curiously. "Eleanor Lawson and Wilfred Bennett."

"They told me what you said to them: Mrs. Lawson on the two occasions she saw you, and Wilfred Bennett just during the interview with the whole family yesterday. I must say, Richard, you were sailing extremely close to the wind."

"Did they also say I made it perfectly clear at yesterday's meeting that I was acting on my own initiative, not on behalf of the bank."

"No, I don't think either of them mentioned that. But it wasn't really relevant. You're an officer of the bank; you can't divorce yourself into two personalities."

"I don't agree with you, sir. I'm responsible for my own actions—"

"Certainly you are," Jarvis agreed. "I'm glad to hear you admit it."

"—and I felt it was my duty to let them know certain facts that might have influenced their decisions. As it happened they weren't influenced and that's all there is to it."

"Not quite all, I think. You're talking about facts, Richard, but what you had was some quite unprovable surmise. We shall have to wait and see what the results of your intervention may be."

"You mean, whether all these people withdraw their accounts from the bank in a body," said Richard bluntly.

"I mean exactly that. You may pray that isn't the outcome of your interference, because if it is, I think my colleagues may be inclined to take a serious view of the matter."

"I see. It doesn't matter to you at all, does it? The fact that Jock Thorold didn't make a will, and consequently Malcolm hasn't a hope of getting the inheritance intended for him, is the old man's own fault, of course, but the family could so easily have made good his intentions—at least so far as to see the boy through his exams.''

"You're quite right in pointing out that it doesn't matter to me," Jarvis told him. "Nor should it to you. May I ask what you intend to do now?"'

"If you mean, am I going to try my hand at any more. . .interference was your word, wasn't it? No, I'm not, but only because I don't think it would do the slightest good.''

"Well, that's a relief at any rate. As a matter of fact," said Jarvis thoughtfully, "I don't really see what else you could do, in the way of investigating Malcolm Stonor's parentage. I expect that's really what you mean, isn't it?''

"Pretty much. So, like you, I shall just have to wait and see what all these good people intend to do.''

"Wait and pray," Jarvis advised him again dryly. "That's all for the moment, Richard. There's a meeting of the joint general managers on Thursday," he added as Richard was already on his way to the door. "We may require your attendance.''

"If you do you know where to find me," said Richard, and closed the door behind him with something of a snap.

II

THERE WERE THINGS that needed to be caught up with on his desk, one or two tricky matters that required discussion with John Kent. It was rather later than usual when Richard left the building in Gracechurch Street to walk home. As he went his mind was busy. The flat in Eden Place was comfortable and convenient, and that evening it had taken on in his eyes some of the attributes of a refuge. His friend, over luncheon in the executive dining room, had listened in silence to an account of his doings during the last few days, and then told him bluntly he was a fool to jeopardize his own position for a boy he'd never seen before. "Whether there's any such outcome as Jarvis envisages or not," said John Kent, "it's going to affect your future. When it's a question of getting a branch—"

"Maggie told me once that it would be bound to be in a small country town," said Richard, as philosophically as he could.

"You mean that's what she'd like?"

"No, I don't think so. It wouldn't be as strange to her as it would be to me, because she was brought up in a place like that, but she's perfectly happy to go wherever I'm sent, or says she is. No, she was meaning my whole attitude toward banking and its conventions. It isn't the first time I haven't seen eye to eye with the general managers, you know."

"I'm quite aware of that, but it would be a dreadful waste. You know perfectly well," said John, who had no false pride, but no assumed humility either, "that it's only the brightest of us that are moved through the Advance Department, to be groomed for stardom more or less. But perhaps if you keep your nose clean for the next year or two. . . . I don't think they'd consider such an appointment until you're in your mid-forties anyway—"

"And if Jock Thorold's descendants and their husbands don't move their accounts in the meantime," said Richard. "I may not be here at all by this time next week."

All this was going through his mind as he walked. He was thinking that after Ricky was safely in bed he'd have to have a long talk with Maggie. He could rely on her to put things into perspective for him, and though she might be worried, they'd been sharing things for fifteen or sixteen years now, and he didn't see any way of avoiding it. He was so preoccupied that the sight of his younger son in the hall when he opened the door of the flat came almost as a surprise to him, though he should have realized that Ricky, who was interested in everything, would long since have concluded that his lateness had some sinister connotation.

"I knew you weren't telling me everything, daddy," said Ricky accusingly. He was practically dancing with excitement. "You said it was just business, nothing to do with the police, but that detective is here again. I just knew you were helping him!"

Richard raised his eyes and saw Maggie standing in the living-room door. "He's quite right, Richard," she said in a rather strained tone. "It's Chief Inspector Denby. He wants a few words with you."

That was so surprising that it silenced Richard for a moment. He was taken up with his own troubles, and they didn't include a visit from the C.I.D. "I don't understand," he said after a moment, rather feebly.

"I expect he'll tell you," said Maggie practically.

"Is he in there? I'll take him into the study," Richard offered.

"No, don't do that. You know it's hideously uncomfortable," said Maggie. "Besides, Ricky and I will be getting supper ready, so you can have your talk with Inspector Denby in peace. Sergeant Axtell is with him, of course," she went on as she made room for Richard to go past her in the doorway.

Richard paused to bestow a kiss on the tip of her nose in passing, a thing he wouldn't ordinarily have done in the circumstances, but he was conscious of a feeling of guilt, even though he was aware this was irrational. Then he turned to face the visitors, and closed the door firmly against Ricky's in-

quisitiveness. "You're the last people I expected to
see," he remarked. And then, remembering his
manners, "Good afternoon, Chief Inspector; good
afternoon, Sergeant."

Detective Chief Inspector Denby was a big man,
on the good-looking side if you overlooked the fact
that he was balding—his graying hair in fact was no
more than a fringe round his head now—and that
the heaviness of his jowls gave him an almost bull-
doglike look of determination. He also wore very
heavy horn-rimmed glasses, which Richard at first
had thought might be for effect; they were certainly formidable enough. But since then he had
realized they were a very necessary remedy for
shortsightedness. "I take it you haven't read the
evening papers yet, Mr. Trenton," said Denby in a
rumbling tone.

"No, I haven't. But why should you assume
that?"

It was Axtell who replied, rather to Richard's surprise. The sergeant was a much younger man, and
of a very different type. He was smaller and slighter
than his superior officer, dark haired and very well
turned out, and with a pair of mild brown eyes.
Richard had never been able to decide whether
these reflected his true character or not; in their
short acquaintance he had come to realize that Axtell was a silent man. Or else, perhaps, that Denby
demanded silence of his subordinates. "Because,"
said the sergeant now, "if you *had* seen the papers
you'd know why we're here."

Half a dozen ideas immediately chased themselves through Richard's mind. One of the branches
had been robbed. Certainly it wasn't the City
branch, which joined head office, and anyway, why
should that bring the police here even if it was one
in his section? Or something might have happened
to Maggie's mother, generally known in the family

as Grandma Maynard; that would hardly be front-
page news. Both Denby and Axtell seemed to be
waiting for him to speak. He looked from one of
them to the other. "Enlighten me," he said.

"It might be as well," said Denby, taking
command of the situation easily, "if we all sat
down."

"Certainly. I'm forgetting my manners, Chief Inspector, but I didn't realize you'd be staying more
than a moment or two. As it seems this may take
some time, may I offer you a drink?"

"It will not only take some time," said Denby, sitting down rather heavily, "it is also official
business. So, though I've no doubt the sergeant
would like to accept your hospitality, I'm afraid
neither of us can do so."

"Have it your own way." Both visitors were
seated now, and Richard crossed the room to take
his own accustomed chair. "I'm afraid I still don't
understand, though. What official business can you
possibly have with me?"

"I understand you have been spending your time
the last few days in making some inquiries that
were nothing directly to do with your employ-
ment."

"Now how on earth could you know that?"

"You're not denying it?"

"No, why should I? But they're nothing at all to
do with you. There's no crime involved, only a
rather incomprehensible piece of negligence on the
part of an old man who recently died intestate.
Nothing to concern the police."

Axtell opened his mouth to reply to that and was
silenced by a look from Denby. "Considering your
activities in the past," said the chief inspector, "I
think it should come as no surprise to you that I'm
interested in what you're doing now."

"That should be in the past tense, Chief Inspector. I've done all I can, and as far as I'm concerned the matter is closed. Though I can't say I like the situation.''

Axtell muttered something this time that sounded like, ''You'll like it still less in a moment.'' He seemed to be in a rebellious mood.

''I should like you to tell me,'' said Denby impressively, ignoring his younger colleague, ''exactly what started you on this quest, and what you know about Mr. Jock Thorold's affairs.''

''Mr. Thorold is dead,'' said Richard, a rather ingenuous remark, which he regretted immediately.

Denby snapped back at him, ''I'm well aware of the fact. I just want you to tell me—''

''He died a natural death, didn't he?'' said Richard, suddenly uneasy. Not that I'd put anything past those daughters of his, he added to himself, but there was nothing to suggest they weren't genuinely fond of their father.

''So far as I'm aware,'' said Denby. ''Why should you jump to the conclusion that anything was wrong?''

''Because of your presence here. That's your job, isn't it, investigating murders?''

''If you remember, Mr. Trenton, I asked you for an account of *your* activities.''

''I know you did, but I'm damned if I'm going to give you one until you explain why I should.''

''Must you be obstructive?''

''I think in this case I must,'' said Richard firmly. ''Unless you give me some idea why I should answer your questions, I don't see why I should oblige you.''

''Very well, then.'' Denby's tone was ominous. ''In the course of these investigations of yours you met Mrs. Geraldine Fielding, I believe. She was murdered last night.''

That silenced Richard for a moment. ''I'm sorry to

hear that, of course," he said, "though I hardly knew her. I believe they had quite a large family, which only makes it worse. But her death could have nothing to do with the matter I was inquiring into."

"Are you so sure of that?"

"I don't see how there could be any connection."

"We'll make a deal with you," said Axtell, who was full of surprises that day. "Tell us what we want to know, and then perhaps we'll explain."

In spite of the shock he had suffered Richard was conscious of amusement. "Perhaps?" he queried gently.

Axtell's answering smile was attractive. "I'm sure you'll find the chief inspector very ready to be reasonable," he said.

Richard wasn't so sure of that, but he said, "Very well," and turned back to Denby, who had been fuming in the background while this exchange was going on. "It started with a small errand that Mr. Jarvis, who is one of our general managers, wanted me to carry out on behalf of the bank," he said.

"What was this errand, as you call it?"

"I'm afraid, to explain that, I have to go back a bit. How much do you know about the family of the late Mr. Thorold, Chief Inspector?"

"A good deal by now," Denby informed him.

And Axtell added helpfully, "We were both up all night."

"I'm sorry to hear it. Then you know—"

"We know that he had three daughters, of whom Mrs. Fielding was the second in order of seniority," said Denby. "They're all married and are all on the comfortable side financially," he added, rather as though he found this a cause for grievance.

"Yes, that's very true. And about Mr. Thorold . . . he was a self-made man, extremely wealthy as I understand it. And he had a protégé, a young man whom he took into his home five years ago, Malcolm Stonor.''

"We know all about Malcolm Stonor,'' said Denby coldly. "And I have heard this and that about your activities, Mr. Trenton—''

"Then I hardly need go into them again,'' said Richard hopefully.

"—but I don't understand what your interest in him is.''

"There was never any formal adoption, you know, and Mr. Thorold had made no promises to the young man, except to see him through his articles as a solicitor, though I think he had given Mr. Fulford, the senior partner of the firm he is with, to understand he intended to set him up in practice for himself once he had qualified. However, Mr. Jock Thorold had spoken to his branch manager, who is by way of being a friend of his, and told him quite categorically that he intended to make a will leaving Malcolm Stonor the clothing factory in Leeds that had been the basis of his fortunes. I understand from talking to Mr. Lawson that this would have constituted about one fourth of the estate. Mr. Blake, the branch manager I spoke of, was already aware that the family intended to do nothing for Malcolm Stonor, and though he realized that in the absence of a will it was quite hopeless to expect that Thorold's full wishes would be honored, he felt that advising them of this fact might persuade them at least to do something for the boy. Continue his allowance, for instance, until he qualified.''

"I find it a little puzzling,'' said Denby slowly, "that you were assigned to this task. It seems this Mr. Blake you speak of would have been the obvious person.''

"Ah, but the trouble is most of these people, the Lawsons, the Fieldings and the Bennetts, kept their

private accounts at least at the Hampstead branch
of our bank. In fact, I think that Fielding, who is an
architect, and Bennett, who is a builder and contractor, keep their business accounts there, as well.
So it would be better if Bob Blake were not personally involved in a matter that might cause offense,
and my general manager also felt that someone
from head office might be more appropriate."

"Someone with tact," said Denby thoughtfully.
"Now, I'd never have thought of that as a description for you, Mr. Trenton."

"Nor I, but I had no choice but to carry out the
commission. Mr. Lawson was obviously in favor of
doing something for young Stonor; in fact I think if
he could have got the rest of the family's permission
he'd have taken Bob Blake's word for it and carried
out Jock Thorold's intentions. But it's his wife and
her sisters who were the interested parties; he had
no choice but to follow their wishes. That was why I
went to see Eleanor Lawson after I left him."

"With what result?"

"No result at all as far as getting any concessions
for Malcolm Stonor." Richard hesitated and then
smiled in spite of himself. "To tell you the truth,
Chief Inspector, I came away furiously angry, and
determined to do what I could to make the family
see reason. But I must stress that what I did after
that was during the weekend, on my own time,
nothing to do with my original instructions from the
bank."

"From which I gather," said Denby shrewdly,
"that some complaint was made, as a result of
which you found yourself, shall we say, unpopular
this morning."

"Yes, that's perfectly true," Richard acknowledged ruefully. "However—"

"As a matter of interest, what did you think you
could do?" asked Denby curiously.

"When I talked to Mr. Fulford we both felt it was most likely that Malcolm Stonor was Thorold's natural son. I thought that if this could be proved, or even suggested strongly, it might make a difference to the way the family looked on him. So I went up to Leeds, where he had lived with his mother, Lilian Stonor, until the time of her death."

"Still furiously angry?" asked Denby curiously.

"Sufficiently so to be quite determined to do what I could. Besides, I'd met Malcolm Stonor and I liked him."

"Impulsive as ever," Denby sighed. "And if you had got the proof you were looking for, what was Stonor going to do?"

"He wouldn't have done anything. He'd never got on with the family and would make no claims on them, and he was grateful to Jock Thorold and didn't feel the old man owed him a thing."

"Then what did you hope to gain?"

"To put it bluntly, I thought I might shame the family into doing something for him. I didn't think it would work with Eleanor, but perhaps the others might be able to persuade her."

"And how did your inquiries go?"

"My informant was a Mrs. Margaret Welford, who lives a few doors away from the Stonors' old house. They had been good friends, she and Lilian Stonor, and up to a point she'd been in Lilian's confidence."

"What did you learn?" asked Denby again.

"That Lilian Stonor, though she called herself Mrs. Stonor, admitted to her friend she had never been married. They were neighbors for fifteen years, since just before Malcolm was born. Mrs. Stonor would leave him with her friend when she went away periodically. According to Mrs. Welford, these disappearances—though that seems rather a strong word—coincided with Jock Thorold's visits

to the factory. He visited Lilian a number of times
during the last six months of her life when she was
too ill to work. Malcolm had already told me that
there never seemed to be any shortage of money,
but I couldn't find out anything about where her
funds had come from.''

"And nothing about a possible affaire before
Malcolm Stonor was born?''.

"I'm afraid it's true. All the same—''

"It's not proof," said Denby, shaking his head.
"Your friend, Mr. Fulford, would have told you
that.''

"I knew it already myself," Richard told him.
"All the same, I thought it was a strong enough
presumption of parenthood for me to put it before
the family for their consideration. Jock Thorold had
told Mrs. Welford that he meant to adopt the boy.
That never got done, I daresay because of the bitter
opposition of his daughters.''

"So you came back and called a conference of the
whole family and laid this so-called information
before them?''

"I did. And, as you undoubtedly know already,
Chief Inspector, without any result at all. Mrs.
Fielding, I think, was genuinely shocked at the suggestion that her father might have had an extramarital affaire.''

"And the others?''

"Philip Lawson was unhappier than ever about
the whole thing, but there was nothing he could do
about it. His son, Phil, sympathizes with his father's
point of view. Eleanor Lawson, I call her the dog-in-
the-manger type, and so for that matter is Wilfred
Bennett—he's the one with the influence in that
household, I should say.''

"You haven't mentioned Maxwell Fielding,"
Denby prompted him.

"No, he was the sort of person it's hard to get an opinion about. But it wasn't his decision, it was his wife's; I daresay he'd have gone along with anything she decided."

"And so—"

"And so I came away; there was nothing more that I could do. As you surmised, I had already exceeded my instructions."

"I understand, though, that your interest in Malcolm Stonor didn't stop there."

"I don't know quite what you mean."

"You found him a place to live, in this very building."

"Oh, yes, I knew there was a studio empty on the ground floor. The rent isn't very much, and he was pleased about it because it would save his fares. Mr. Fulford is giving him a job, you know. But I don't suppose it will pay very much while he's in training."

"I see. When did he come into residence?"

"I understand from Phil Lawson, who visited us last night, that he'd moved in the afternoon. Phil and another friend, a girl called Joanna Martin, had come to see him, a sort of housewarming. But as he was out they came up here instead."

"And what time was this?"

"Just after nine o'clock, as far as I remember." Richard paused before he went on. "I've answered all your questions patiently, Chief Inspector," he said then. "And, of course, I can see you'd want to know about my dealings with the family, since I saw them all so recently. But you must also see that Malcolm Stonor's affairs, and my connection with them, can have nothing whatever to do with Mrs. Fielding's death."

"You think not, Mr. Trenton?"

"Of course I do! But it sounded suspiciously as if

you were looking for an alibi for Malcolm, or perhaps hoping that he wouldn't have one. What has the family been saying about him?''

''Their opinion of him is much as you described it to me, Mr. Trenton. It has nothing to do with my interest in his movements. And Mr. Lawson, Jr., has already told me that he found Mr. Stonor out at nine o'clock yesterday evening, though he had returned home by half-past ten.''

''Well, of course, Phil would tell you that if you asked him, but what have Malcolm's movements to do with you?''

''A great deal, Mr. Trenton, a great deal.'' Denby looked as if he was on the point of getting to his feet when Sergeant Axtell made another of his unexpected interventions.

''Don't you think it might be a good idea to explain matters to Mr. Trenton, sir?'' he asked. ''If he understood the position he might be able to be even more helpful.''

The chief inspector sank back into his chair again. ''Well, now, that's a thought,'' he said slowly, and equally slowly a smile spread over his face. ''Perhaps I will tell you after all,'' he said. There was absolutely no doubt in Richard's mind that whatever Denby's motive was, it was malicious. ''You're always so ready to believe we're in the wrong, Mr. Trenton. It might do you some good to look at the matter from our point of view,'' the detective went on.

Richard would have liked to say, ''I've no real desire to look at the matter at all,'' and speed them on their way. But his curiosity got the better of him, and he had another even more compelling reason for wanting to hear what Denby had to say. In view of Geraldine Fielding's death he had seen no reason not to be frank with Denby, but if he had succeeded in giving a wrong impression.... ''What are you going to tell me, Chief Inspector?'' he asked in a rather strained tone.

Denby answered his question with another. ''Where do you think Mrs. Fielding's body was found?'' he inquired.

8

"How ON EARTH should I know?" Richard was indignant. "At her home, I suppose, or somewhere near it."

"She was in a flat in Mayfair rented to a Mr. and Mrs. Hector Peabody," said Denby with an air of quiet satisfaction. "It's on the ground floor, and one of the other tenants noticed that the front door was ajar as he passed. As it was getting late, nearly eleven o'clock by that time, he thought it might be due to an oversight, and knocked to attract their attention. When he got no reply he pushed the door a little and went in a few steps to call out and try again to attract someone's attention. What he saw was the poor lady's feet sticking out from behind the sofa."

"What had happened to her?"

"Her skull had been crushed in by the traditional blunt instrument," said Denby. Oddly, he seemed to be enjoying himself. "In this case the figure of a bronze elephant, which the maid who cleaned the flat once a week said had been used as a doorstop."

"Well, surely . . . what was she doing there? What had Mr. and Mrs. Peabody to say about that?"

"That brings us to the oddest point of all," the chief inspector told him. "The fellow tenant who found the body identified it as Mrs. Peabody."

"Then I don't understand at all," said Richard, shaking his head.

"What don't you understand, Mr. Trenton?"

"Well, for one thing, if you thought she was Mrs. Peabody, how did you come to identify her as Geraldine Fielding?"

"That was quite simple. Her handbag was in the flat and there was plenty of identification there. The man who found her, whose name is Weatherby, said he encountered her sometimes in the late afternoon leaving the flat. The maid, who always went in the morning, had never seen either of her employers at all. Her money was left for her in an envelope regularly every Tuesday. Another of the tenants saw her very occasionally, but that was all."

"What about Mr. Peabody?"

"He was equally elusive—even more so in fact. Nobody would admit to ever having seen him."

"What about the rental office?"

"The arrangements had been made by telephone. They weren't too surprised about that; they are luxury flats and people often take them for short terms. As it happens this particular tenancy has gone on for more than two years. The rent was paid quarterly by a check on your own Mayfair branch, Mr. Trenton. The account was a joint one in the names of Hector and Mavis Peabody, and the lady had always signed the check. As it happens the bank was glad about this; the specimen signature Mr. Peabody gave them was no more than a line with a couple of humps in it, which they felt would have been easy to forge. We've had our experts on to Mavis Peabody's signature, and there's no doubt that it was written by Geraldine Fielding."

"When was the account opened?"

"Just before the flat was rented. It was opened by a deposit of one thousand pounds in cash, and subsequent deposits have always been in cash, too. I spoke to the clerk who dealt with the matter, but he can't remember anything about either of the people concerned—I mean about their appearance. It was a quite routine matter, and there was nothing extraordinary about them in any way.''

"So you're quite sure that Mavis Peabody—they chose a couple of comic names for themselves, didn't they?—and Geraldine Fielding are one and the same person.''

"Absolutely sure.''

"And nobody ever saw Hector Peabody?''

"Not that I can find out. What does that sound like to you, Mr. Trenton?''

"I suppose,'' said Richard reluctantly, "it sounds like what the newspapers used to call a love nest.''

"Precisely. But you tell me that Mrs. Fielding was the one of Jock Thorold's daughters who was genuinely shocked by the idea that he might have had an illegitimate son.''

"That was my impression certainly,'' said Richard. "But people are queer, you know. Inconsistent,'' he added, as though he might not have made his meaning quite clear.

"I'm only too well aware of the fact,'' said Denby dryly.

"I mean, it might be filial feeling, or affection for her mother, or something like that that was behind her attitude.''

"In other words,'' said Axtell, "she might not feel that what was sauce for the gander was necessarily sauce for the goose.''

"That was more or less what I had in mind, Sergeant. How long did it take to get the poor woman properly identified?''

"No longer than it took the investigating officer to look through her handbag,'' said Denby.

"Do any of her family know who Peabody is?''

"If they do they're not admitting it. But there's something else that was found in the flat that I

think might interest you, Mr. Trenton: Jock
Thorold's will.''

This time Richard was completely silenced for a
moment. ''Everybody thought he died intestate,''
he said then, weakly. ''Do you mean to say that
Geraldine had this will all the time?''

''It seems as if that must have been the case. Do
you see where this leads us, I wonder?''

''How can I? You haven't given me enough to go
on. What did the will say?''

''I suppose I may as well tell you, as your friend
Mr. Blake certainly will if I don't,'' said Denby. ''He
is named as executor. It's a holograph will. No harm
in that—the old boy was clever enough from all I
hear to make sure there were no errors in it. And
the bequests are exactly as you described them: the
clothing factory to Malcolm Stonor and the residue
of the estate divided equally among his three
daughters.''

''Does he name Stonor as his own son?''

''No, nothing like that.''

''Well, I still don't see. . . it's a complete mystery
how Mrs. Fielding could have come by the will, or
why she should have kept it at all if she wanted to
suppress it. But in the circumstances it's perfectly
obvious what you must do.''

''And what is that?'' asked Denby almost indul-
gently, but Richard was in no doubt that there was
some sarcasm behind the words.

''Find Peabody, of course. Not that I suppose for a
moment that that's his name.''

''No, I don't suppose so, either.''

''Are there any fingerprints in the flat?'' asked
Richard suddenly.

''A few, of Mrs. Fielding's. It was cleaned thoroughly yesterday, and perhaps the man hasn't been
there since.''

''But surely. . . toilet articles, things like that.''

"There were towels and soap, of course, but no razor or toothbrushes. Nothing to indicate that anyone had ever spent the night there."

"Merely a place of rendezvous," said Richard slowly. "Even so—"

"There's 'one difficulty about your theory, Mr. Trenton," Denby told him. "Mrs. Fielding was there yesterday, but I understand from what I have learned of her movements in general that this must have been unusual in the evening. But there's nothing at all to show that Mr. Peabody, whoever he is, was there, too."

"But it's obvious—"

"Not obvious at all," Denby retorted. "You see, there's one fact I haven't told you yet. Your young friend, Malcolm Stonor, was there, between half-past nine and ten o'clock. He was one of the first people we questioned after we found the will, and he admits that quite freely."

"That—" Richard broke off and looked from one to the other of his companions rather wildly. "Even if Malcolm wanted to see her, and I should imagine that was the last thing he'd want to do, how would he know where to find her?"

"I think you must ask him all that yourself, Mr. Trenton," said Denby. "I've been remarkably frank with you, as I'm sure you'll admit. Have you anything more to tell me?"

"Nothing at all. I'm completely . . . completely befuddled by the whole thing," said Richard. Then a sudden thought struck him. "You didn't find any fingerprints on this elephant affair?" he asked.

"Only Mrs. Fielding's, considerably smudged. Somebody held it in a handkerchief, perhaps, and used the flat side, the surface it stood on, to hit her. And then to hit her again," he added, watching Richard's expression.

Richard, to tell the truth, was beginning to feel

rather sick: "You're describing somebody blind with anger," he said.

"I think that's a fair enough description."

"But why should Malcolm Stonor...even if he wanted to see Mrs. Fielding, which I don't believe, why should he go to this Mayfair flat to find her?"

"I think I've said enough, Mr. Trenton."

"At least you see now," said Sergeant Axtell, "why we wanted to know what you found out about his background. The will turning up like that."

"You're saying it ties him in with the murder. I don't believe that, either."

"I'm afraid you may have to come to believe it," said Denby. This time he did get to his feet, and Axtell followed suit. "You see, Mr. Trenton, we made another call in this building on our way here. Malcolm Stonor has been charged with murder."

"Does Jake Fulford know?" asked Richard quickly.

"As far as I know, Mr. Fulford is generally on his way home at this time of the evening. No, he doesn't know yet, unless Stonor has succeeded in reaching him from the police station."

"Has he made a statement...Malcolm, I mean?"

"No statement."

"It seems he's profited from his training in a solicitor's office," Sergeant Axtell put in. "He declined to say a word until he had advice."

"Well, good for him!"

"For a law-abiding citizen, Mr. Trenton, that's a very odd reaction."

"I told you I didn't believe he'd done it. There must be some explanation; you'll hear it when he gets in touch with Fulford. Meanwhile—"

"Yes, Mr. Trenton?"

That was said coldly and Richard laughed again. "Oh, I wasn't going to tell you I was continuing my investigation, Chief Inspector,'' he said. ''Nothing like that. I don't see that there's anything I can do.''

''I'm relieved to hear it. What were you going to say?''

''I was going to advise you to look a little further for your murderer than you seem to have done already.''

''Ah, yes, the elusive Mr. Peabody.''

''Well, I think you ought to find out who he is. I'll tell you one thing, Chief Inspector, Jock Thorold was a firm believer in a husband supporting his wife. He didn't make his daughters' allowances after they were married. So whoever was financing this Mayfair flat, it wasn't Mrs. Fielding herself.''

''You're telling me Mr. Peabody may be an important person. That doesn't help, I'm afraid. However, we must be going, and I must say you've relieved my mind considerably. I don't want to be falling over you at every turn we take. If you'll apologize to Mrs. Trenton for us for our having kept you so long—'' He was on the way to the door as he spoke with the sergeant at his heels. Richard followed them into the hall and a moment later, their farewells having been said, closed the front door behind them. He wasn't surprised to turn from that task to find Ricky standing on one leg in the kitchen doorway.

''There you see, daddy,'' he said. ''I knew it had something to do with the police again. He wants your help, doesn't he?''

''On the contrary,'' said Richard dryly, his eyes meeting Maggie's over his son's head, ''he warned me off in no uncertain terms. But it's no use looking anxious about it, Maggie. There's nothing to be done anyway. For goodness sake, come into the living room and let's have a drink.''

Ricky followed them. ''But there has been a murder,'' he persisted.

Richard looked helplessly at his wife. "You may as well tell us, Richard, darling," said Maggie surprisingly. "If you're thinking about Ricky, he's far more likely to have a sleepless night out of sheer frustration than to have nightmares over even the most gruesome details."

This was only too true. Ricky, besides, was a well-adjusted child. "You're quite right, old son," said Richard, seating himself. "A woman I was talking to only yesterday has been killed, which is why Chief Inspector Denby wanted to talk to me. But that's the end of my connection with the case."

Maggie had gone across the room to pour sherry for herself and a stiffer whiskey than usual for her husband. "Would you like some soda, Ricky?" she asked over her shoulder.

"Yes, that would be lovely, mummy. But why did you go to see this lady?" Ricky insisted.

"Oh, she's a client of the bank," said Richard vaguely. He might have known, however, that his son was not to be put off so easily.

"It's all to do with this business you say has been occupying you all the weekend," said Ricky severely. "Isn't that right?"

"Denby thinks it is," Richard admitted. "But I don't agree with him."

Maggie had finished her ministrations and came to sit down. "Make him tell us who was killed, mummy," Ricky demanded.

"Her name was Geraldine Fielding," said Richard, "and you're none the wiser now I've told you."

"Who did it?"

"I don't know."

"But you're going to find out, aren't you, daddy?"

"Certainly not. I told you my connection with the affair was quite over."

"Yes, you *said* that." Ricky fixed his father with a stern eye. "Can you tell me, daddy, cross your heart and hope to die, that you're not going to do one single thing more about what happened?"

"Well—" said Richard. Ricky, who had been seated precariously on the edge of his chair, got up suddenly, spilling a little of his soda.

"There, you see!" he said triumphantly. "It's no good trying to pull the wool over our eyes, is it, mummy?"

"No good at all," Maggie agreed, torn between amusement and the tinge of anxiety that was part of her nature.

"Just one telephone call," Richard asserted. "I think I owe Jake Fulford that much. After that, Ricky, it will be all over as far as we are concerned."

"But you said you don't agree with Chief Inspector Denby."

"No, I don't agree with him at all."

"Well," said Ricky, consideringly, "I daresay you're telling me the truth as it seems to you now, but you'll change your mind, I know you will. You wouldn't like to see the chief inspector make a fool of himself, would you, daddy?"

At that Richard burst out laughing, which to Maggie at least conveyed as good an answer as any other. "That's enough of that, Ricky," he said, getting up. "I'll make that telephone call, and when I come back I don't want to hear another word about it."

Jake Fulford was home by then, and just getting over the shock that the news of Malcolm's arrest had given him. "I'll have to attend the magistrate's court tomorrow morning," he told Richard, "but that won't be until eleven o'clock. I'll see Malcolm first thing, so if you could come by my office at nine-thirty, say, I'll tell you—with his permission—

what his explanation is. It seems so strange that he should be calling on Geraldine Fielding at all, and particularly at a place none of the family knew about—or did they?—where she was known as Peabody."

"It does seem strange," Richard agreed, "and I'd be glad to know the answer. Another queer thing is the will turning up. So I'll certainly be on your doorstep at nine-thirty."

They talked for a little while after that, and Richard rejoined his family. Dinner was ready and Ricky, who knew pretty well how far he could go, had no more questions. After he'd gone to bed Richard gave Maggie a few more details about Geraldine Fielding's murder, the mystery of her double identity, and the man who called himself Hector Peabody, whom nobody seemed ever to have seen. "I'm not quite sure what makes Denby so sure of his case," he concluded. "Having a chap like Peabody on the fringe of things must give the defense a lever, I should think. But that's Jake's affair, not mine."

"Will Mr. Fulford try to find him?"

"I don't know. He might put a firm of inquiry agents on to it, I suppose. I believe solicitors make use of them extensively at times. But I'd have thought the mere mention of his name, the fact that the dead woman was apparently conducting an affaire with him, would be quite enough for the reasonable doubt the lawyers talk about."

"Yes, I should have thought that, too," said Maggie in her quiet way. "I don't think that's all you have to tell me, though, is it?"

"What on earth do you mean?"

"Only a conversation I had with Jarvis this morning," said Richard. "It's not worth mentioning."

Maggie thought that out for a moment. "At a guess I should say you mean that one of the people you were talking to yesterday had made a complaint to him, or to one of the other general managers," she said. "How did he take it?" she added, not even waiting for his confirmation of her surmise.

"Badly," said Richard. "There seems to be some suggestion of the wholesale transfer of accounts, but I should say—wouldn't you—that a murder in the family may have distracted them a little from their intention."

"It would certainly distract me," said Maggie, more forcefully than was her custom. "Are you trying to tell me, Richard, that you—your fate hangs in some way on what they do?"

"I suppose it does," said Richard reluctantly. "But Jarvis wouldn't be alone in making a decision like that, you know. He's a contrary sort of bastard, but there are others concerned."

"Then I shouldn't worry about it, Richard, darling," said Maggie, who might worry herself sick over small things but was generally quite unmoved by the major crises of life.

"As a matter of fact, I'm more worried about Malcolm Stonor."

"Yes, you liked him, didn't you? Perhaps Ricky is right and you should try to do something about it."

"I haven't decided yet whether Ricky intends to be a barrister or policeman," said Richard, smiling at her. "But whatever I am it's not a detective, and the fact that chance has thrown me into Denby's path on a couple of occasions doesn't make it any more likely that I could do anything to help."

"I suppose not," said Maggie reluctantly. "It's just that you have a sense of fair play, Richard, darling, and I don't like you to be worried."

9

THE FOLLOWING MORNING Richard made a brief telephone call to the senior of his two assistants in B
section to say that his arrival at the bank would be a
little delayed. After that, reveling in the lack of
hurry, he sat over his coffee with Maggie and
endeavored to reassure her about the possible effects of his actions over the weekend, about which,
however, she still declined to show much concern.
She had always been sensitive to his feelings, and
now they were both well enough aware that a
murder charge was rather more serious than a mere
job, or the possibility of being transferred to work
he did not care for.

The offices of Fulford and Hughes were only two
minutes away down Bread Court, so it was natural
that he was a little late for his appointment.
However, no harm was done; as he went out of the
front door of Eden Place he saw Jake Fulford's tall
figure striding toward him. They met on the doorstep, and Jake led the way up the stairs, talking as
he went. "I thought I'd find you waiting for me,"
he said. "The thing is, I was talking to young
Malcolm longer than I thought."

After that they waited until they were in Fulford's office to go into the matter further, though
Richard was not in the mood to contain his curiosity. "What had Malcolm to say to you?" he demanded, as soon as they were alone together.

Jake, on his own ground now, declined to be hurried. "He left us yesterday afternoon," he said, "to take over the studio apartment that Mrs. Trenton had so kindly found for him. I think, to tell you the truth, that though he was profuse in his thanks to Marcia he was rather excited over the prospect of his own place. Well, what lad of twenty wouldn't be? I took him and his suitcases to the station and left him there."

"Yes, Phil Lawson told me he'd moved in yesterday afternoon," said Richard. "I didn't see him myself, but Phil and a girl called Joanna were looking for him later in the evening."

"I like the sound of that young man," said Jake thoughtfully. "What was the girl like?"

"A very nice girl, as far as I could tell. Friendly and polite, that's about all I could say after such a short acquaintance. But you're quite right about Phil, he was anxious not to take unfair advantage of Malcolm because of his rather more affluent circumstances. That's why he brought the girl with him."

"And which one of them does she favor?" asked Jake curiously.

"What do you think I am? A clairvoyant? I haven't the faintest idea," said Richard. "Anyway, we're off the subject, and being a lawyer I do think you ought to be able to stick to it for two minutes together."

"Yes...well." Jake paused to think it over. "Malcolm says he arrived at Eden Place at about four o'clock, he can't put it nearer than that. He unpacked his bags and admired his surroundings for a while, and then made himself a cup of tea. Did you know, by the way, that Mrs. Trenton had done some grocery shopping for him? He asked me to make sure she was paid for what she bought."

"No, I didn't know, but it's quite like Maggie.

Anyway, that doesn't matter for the moment. Can't you see I'm curious?''

"I can see that all right," said Jake, grinning. "But I shouldn't be teasing you," he added suddenly, "when Malcolm's in so much trouble."

"Perhaps he said he'd rather you didn't talk to me," said Richard. "In that case, of course, I quite understand."

"No, he particularly asked me to tell you."

"Did he know I'd been to Leeds, and had another go at the family after I got back?"

"Yes, I told him."

"Did he... were his conclusions the same as ours?"

"Not being an idiot, he was perfectly well aware of what I thought. However, he told me for the first time that he always felt he must be Jock Thorold's son, and that was the only thing that made him agree to join him five years ago. Jock made the difficulties inherent in the move perfectly clear to him, and I think he had enough imagination to see for himself what they might be. So all the things your Mrs. Welford told you were no real surprise to him. But I think he's telling the truth, Richard, when he says that even if you'd been able to find proof of what we suspect he wouldn't have taken any action to cut himself in on the estate. I might want your evidence on that point when it comes to trial, though now that the will has been found, and he inherits just what Jock told your friend Bob Blake he wanted him to, I'm afraid the jury will think that's easy to say now."

"Yes, I'm afraid so, too. But I'll be quite willing to do anything I can, of course, and like you, I believe he meant what he said. You'd got to him making a cup of tea, Jake, what happened then?"

"The telephone rang—"

"How on earth did anyone know the number?"

"It hadn't been disconnected. Of course it was still under the name of the previous tenant, but Phil Lawson knew what that was. I can only suppose he told the rest of the family, or perhaps Mrs. Fielding asked him particularly."

"Yes, that fits. It was Mrs. Fielding on the phone, then?"

"It certainly was. She gave him her name and told him that certain matters had arisen that she would like to discuss with him. As she had always been particularly cold toward him that surprised him, of course. However, she was Jock's daughter, and as I told you, he suspected she was his half sister also, and he didn't want to be disrespectful to her. So he said, 'All right, I'll come up to Hampstead right away if that suits you.'"

"And did it suit her?"

"No, she said immediately that it wouldn't be convenient. She gave him the address in Mayfair where she was found, and said she'd borrowed the flat from some friends just for this interview because she wanted it to be private. He should come there and ring the bell marked Peabody. And that not before nine-thirty in the evening."

"What did he make of that?"

"It surprised him, naturally. When he thought it over he decided that she wanted to keep whatever she had to say a secret from the rest of the family, but what it could be he hadn't the faintest idea. Anyway, as I've said, he agreed to visit her, arrived outside the block of flats about a quarter of an hour early, and walked about outside until the time she had mentioned came around. Then he went and punched the bell and she let him in herself. He thinks they were alone in the flat together. He certainly saw nobody else, heard no movement, and had the distinct impression from her manner that nobody else was there.''

Jake paused at that point, and after a moment Richard said impatiently, ''Well?''

''Wait for it,'' Jake advised. ''Not that there's much more, at least it isn't very illuminating. She started off as frigidly as usual, Malcolm says, by saying, 'I understand that you're now claiming to be a relative of ours.' And when Malcolm said he was claiming nothing of the sort, she asked whether you, Richard, hadn't visited them at his instigation, and whether it was his intention to try to create a scandal for his own benefit. When he assured her again that he had nothing like that in mind she sniffed unbelievingly—those were Malcolm's own words—and said, 'My sister Alexandra might believe you, she's the credulous one, but I'm afraid I don't.' ''

''That can't have been all.''

''No, it wasn't. As far as I can tell she put him through a pretty stiff cross-examination about his life before he came to Hampstead, about his mother, about their finances, their friends, her occasional absences from home and the name of the woman who used to look after him on those occasions when he was very young. Checking up, as far as I can tell, on what you told the family yourself.''

''That sounds like it certainly, but he must have talked to them before about all that. After all, Malcolm lived with Jock Thorold for five years.''

''But the daughters didn't take any notice of him. At least, perhaps I should say the two eldest ones didn't. I gather from Malcolm that Alexandra sometimes showed a little interest. But on the whole they accepted his presence because they had to, but only acknowledged his existence in the most grudging way. And, of course, this conversation last evening was not without its awkwardness. Malcolm

was well enough aware of how she felt about him,
well aware also that if she came to believe in their
relationship it would be a shock to her, and to do
him justice I don't think he wanted to hurt her in
any way.''

"Well, all I can say," said Richard bluntly, "is
that was exceedingly magnanimous of him. I don't
think any of them, with the exception of Philip
Lawson and his son, have ever cared a scrap for *his*
feelings. Though they must have known it was a
lonely life, however fond he grew of Jock.''

"Yes, but I think he understood their point of
view, too. Three girls from a working-class background whose father made a pile and brought them
to London where they married well. Malcolm was a
continual reminder of their origins, whether he
wanted to be or not. I think perhaps we shouldn't
blame them too much.''

"You'd blame Eleanor fast enough if you'd ever
talked to her, and I'd say the same thing about
Geraldine, except for the old *de mortuis* tag.
Anyway, Jake, she asked him questions and he
answered her as well as he could, but having more
regard than he might have had for her feelings.
What happened when this inquisition finished?''

"He said she'd become very agitated, and was
pacing up and down the room. He felt awkward,
because when he tried to stand up, too, she just
waved him back impatiently into his chair. And he
said there was a dead silence, except that she was
breathing rather heavily, for quite five minutes,
though I take leave to doubt if it was as long as that.
Then she turned on him and said without any warning in a very harsh tone, 'Can you find your own
way out?' "

"Was that all she said? No explanation of her
questions, or what she meant to do about the
answers?''

."Not a thing, Malcolm says. So he got to his feet and said good-night awkwardly and let himself out, and all the time she didn't say another word."

"That's odd. How long had he been there?"

"About half an hour, I think. Anyway, he got home about ten-fifteen and soon after that Phil Lawson and the girl came down from your flat and spent another half hour with him. I shall have to find out how he seemed at that time, but he was at the office all day yesterday and I can vouch myself for the fact that his demeanor was just as usual. He hadn't even heard of the murder when your friend Chief Inspector Denby and a number of satellites called on him. He had the sense to refuse to answer questions until I talked to him, and he was dispatched to the police station under guard. Then I understand that Denby came up to see you."

"Yes, that's right. He told me that Geraldine Fielding had definitely been identified as Mrs. Hector Peabody and the tenant of the apartment where she was found, and also that Jock Thorold's will had turned up there."

"That seems to be right, though I'll know more about the police case after the hearing. It's a puzzling business and I don't know what to make of it."

"Will the fact that the dead woman was apparently conducting a clandestine affaire have any effect on the defense?" asked Richard.

"If there's any justice in the world, it should," said Jake, but not very hopefully. He paused a moment, and then, "Do you believe in Hector Peabody?" he inquired.

"I suppose there was a man who visited the flat, though no one ever seems to have seen him. What point would there have been in maintaining it otherwise? But whether that was his name or not I should think very doubtful."

"My own feeling exactly. In that case, why should the will have been there?"

"That stumps me, too," Richard admitted.

"What did you think of Geraldine Fielding?" Jake asked.

"I thought she was genuinely shocked by the possibility that Malcolm was her illegitimate brother. That shows how wrong you can be, doesn't it? I mean, if she was committing adultery herself all the time."

"You never know with people," said Jake. "She might have been shocked by the idea of her father having an affaire, if she idealized him for instance, but felt it was quite a different thing for her to do so."

"That's much what I said myself last night. People are contradictory, there's no getting away from it. She was certainly an attractive woman, though not a patch on her elder sister. But wouldn't you have thought her husband and her four children would have kept her fully occupied?"

"That's an exceedingly ingenuous remark, if I may say so," said Jake, amused. "Is there any chance of your attending the magistrates' court hearing? It might answer a few more of your questions if you do."

"Not a hope. I've got to get to the bank, and in any case I've been warned off by Jarvis, that's the one of the general managers, who generally acts as a spokesman for the whole body. It's as much as my life's worth to interfere any further."

"That's a pity," said Jake, "you seem to have an aptitude for that sort of thing."

"Not you, too," said Richard in heartfelt tones.

"What do you mean by that?"

"Only that my young son has got it into his head that I'm the modern personification of all the great detectives of fiction. An impression that I could well do without; he's enough of a handful already. But as for satisfying my curiosity, Jake—"

"Call in on your way home from the office to-night. I'll wait for you if you like. Then I can tell you exactly what went on at the hearing."

II

IT WAS NOT the most pleasant of surprises for Richard when he arrived in his own room a lit-tle later to find Edward Jarvis already there and waiting for him. Characteristically, Mr. Jarvis had made himself completely at home, but he had not actually occupied Richard's own chair behind the desk. He didn't move when his subordi-nate came in, merely raised a hand in a rather halfhearted greeting and said bluntly, "You're late."

"So I am," said Richard mildly. And then, "You told me, sir, that your next meeting was on Thurs-day."

Jarvis waved this remark aside as if it was of lit-tle account. "Have you heard what's happened, Richard?" he asked.

There was only one subject uppermost in Richard's mind: not his own future but the puzzling events of Sunday evening. "If you mean Mrs. Geraldine Fielding's death, yes, I have heard about it. Chief Inspector Denby came to see me last night. Like you, he was concerned about my investiga-tions during the weekend."

"But not, I imagine, for the same reason," said Jarvis dryly.

"Not exactly, though he looks on them with no greater favor than you do."

"Well, as to that, I'm disposed to let bygones be bygones."

"You imagine that Mrs. Fielding's death will

make a difference to the family's feelings about their accounts,'' said Richard bluntly.

"I do more than imagine it, I'm quite sure of it. Philip Lawson phoned me late yesterday, with his wife's permission, to say that in view of the discovery of the will they were disposed to be sympathetic toward your actions.''

"Meaning, I suppose,'' said Richard bitterly, "that they hadn't believed a word I said to them before.''

"That may be so. I'm more disposed to think that it merely made the bank's concern seem more reasonable to them.''

"I'm surprised they were thinking about things like that at all in the circumstances,'' said Richard.

"Perhaps you're forgetting that Bob Blake is the executor of Jock Thorold's will,'' Jarvis pointed out.

"No, I can see that could make a difference. But Lawson can't have known when he spoke to you, and you may not have heard of it yourself, sir. Malcolm Stonor is now under arrest for Mrs. Fielding's murder.''

Edward Jarvis's eyes were closed almost to slits. "Are you telling me the truth, Richard?'' he asked.

"Certainly I am. What possible motive could I have for lying? Apparently it was the finding of the will that sent the police to see him, and he admitted quite readily that he had visited her at the Mayfair flat on Sunday evening, leaving her approximately an hour before her dead body was found. I don't know what the police theory is, or what other evidence they may have in their possession. But if his guilt is proved and he goes to prison, Jock's will will make very little difference to him.''

"That's very interesting.''

"Yes, I thought you might find it so. For myself I find it distressing.''

"You met the boy, didn't you? What did you think of him?"

"That he's quite incapable of doing a thing like that."

"Can any evidence of that be adduced, I wonder?"

"I don't know, but there's a good deal of mystery surrounding the circumstances of Geraldine Fielding's death. The flat in which she was killed was rented by a Mr. and Mrs. Hector Peabody, and there seems no doubt that she was the Mrs. Peabody concerned. I should imagine myself that the defense could quite easily interest the jury in the identity of Hector Peabody, who—if there was a liaison, as we must assume—was apparently even more discreet about it than she was."

"You're trying to tell me that she was seen occasionally but he wasn't."

"That's it exactly."

"Then how do we know he exists at all?"

"I can't see any other reason for Mrs. Fielding taking the flat, or putting it in the two names for that matter."

"How was the rent paid?"

"By check, signed Mavis Peabody in Geraldine Fielding's writing, and drawn on our Mayfair branch. But I don't need to remind you, sir, that the account could have been opened without the man appearing at all. She'd only to take the necessary specimen signature forms away with her and return them later. Nobody would have been any the wiser."

"I agree with you, of course, but I also agree that it would seem an unlikely course of conduct. Why did Stonor go there on Sunday, and how did he know where to go?"

"He went at her request, and she told him she had borrowed the apartment for their interview. He was there for about half an hour and she questioned him closely about his life in Leeds, going over, in fact, all the things I had told the family that afternoon. He said she seemed agitated when they had finished talking, but then she asked him to leave, which he did. That's absolutely all I know. The magistrates' court hearing is this morning, and something else may emerge then.''

Edward Jarvis got up and took a turn about the room. ''I've come to have a certain respect for your instinct in these matters, Richard,'' he said.

Richard followed his movements with his eyes. ''That's rather a change of tune, isn't it?'' he said, in no mood to appreciate the compliment. ''I think you know as well as I do that it's not my métier, never was and never will be.''·

''You underrate yourself, Richard, I'm sure of that. If Malcolm Stonor is indeed innocent—''

''What then?'' asked Richard suspiciously.

''I'm quite sure you will realize,'' said Jarvis bluntly, coming to a halt at the corner of the desk, ''that the young man might not feel particularly kindly toward us if you were to desert him now.''

''You'd better spell it out for me a little further,'' said Richard. ''I'm not feeling particularly bright this morning.''

''I mean that you should continue your inquiries, what else? There's no reason why you shouldn't; the family is disposed to be conciliatory now.''

''But Chief Inspector Denby isn't. All I can tell you is that he would take the dimmest view of anything I might do in that connection.''

''Ah, but you have a line on the defense. This Mr. Fulford is by way of being a friend of yours, isn't he?''

''He is, but I don't feel disposed to take advantage of the fact.''

''Nonsense, he'll be glad of your help.'' That

silenced Richard for a moment; he had an uncomfortable feeling it was only too true. "Besides, if you really feel young Stonor is innocent, I don't see how you can just let the matter drop," Jarvis added persuasively.

"No, but. . .look here, sir, I'm not at all equipped for this kind of thing. Let the police do their own dirty work."

"But the police, you tell me, are barking up the wrong tree," said Jarvis. "Besides which I have every faith in you."

"That's all very well, but what do you want me to do?" asked Richard rather querulously.

"Why, find Hector Peabody, of course." Jarvis was moving toward the door. "That's the obvious place to begin I should have thought." He went out of the room, closing the door very gently behind him, but a moment later he opened it again and stuck his head in to say, "It's a quiet time of year, Richard; no reason why you shouldn't take a few days off. I'll speak to John Kent about keeping an eye on your section."

III

Richard tidied his desk before he went, and had a word with John Kent, feeling himself rather more familiar with what was going on in B section than even the eminent Mr. Jarvis. John was inclined to be amused by the assignment his friend had been given, but seeing Richard's indignation he wisely kept the emotion to himself. It was nearly lunchtime when they had finished, and Richard took himself home, knowing that even if Maggie wasn't expecting him she'd find something or other for him to eat. She received him calmly, but it wasn't long before he realized that she took his unexpected arrival to mean that he had been summarily dismissed from his position. Several minutes were lost in reassurance, and when he had finished she took his new assignment almost lightly. "You have to admit, darling Richard, that Ricky will be pleased about it," she said.

"Don't you start, too," Richard grumbled. "It's bad enough having that infernal child deciding I'm God's gift to the detective force without having you agree with him."

"But you think Malcolm is innocent," said Maggie. "I really don't see what else you can do."

"And when Denby comes roaring round seeking whom he may devour," said Richard, "who's going to talk to him?"

"You, I expect," said Maggie, who had an honest nature. "But think," she said again, "how pleased Ricky will be."

"Where is he, by the way?"

"He took his lunch to school. There was a rehearsal for the end-of-term play. Something like that."

After that they sat down to beer and ham sandwiches. Richard didn't often drink at lunchtime, but that day he felt it was justified. He told Maggie all about his talk with Jake Fulford, and again, in greater detail, what Edward Jarvis had said to him. "You see, he trusts you," said Maggie when he had finished.

"I don't want to be trusted."

"I mean, he trusts your judgment," she explained. "And also trusts you to do something to back it up."

"Yes, that's what I thought you meant, and I don't see that it makes things any better." Richard declined to be comforted.

"How are you going to start?"

"You heard what I told you Jarvis said: I'm to find Hector Peabody. A man I don't believe exists, not under that name at any rate. So I'm going straight to that address in Mayfair. It's on Bruton Avenue. Jake wrote the number down for me somewhere. And I bet you anything you like, Maggie, that I shan't find out a single thing there. After that I'm going to have another word with Jake, and then I'm coming home. And if Ricky is as full of questions as he was last night I shall probably strangle him,'' he added, but he smiled as he said it so that even Maggie couldn't find much in the statement to alarm her.

10

Bruton Avenue wasn't strictly speaking an avenue at all, but a narrow cul-de-sac with a terrace of rather narrow three-story houses on either side. All were immaculately maintained, and number seventeen, Richard's objective, was no different in this from the others. The front door was open revealing a small porch, and ready to his right hand were three bells, the bottom of which bore the name of Peabody. Obviously it was no good trying that one, so he let his eyes go higher. Beside the top bell was the name Marsh, and beside the middle one the name Weatherby. There was nothing to indicate whether the flats concerned were occupied by one person or by a family, though Richard remembered that Weatherby had been the name of the man who had found Mrs. Peabody, so he pressed that bell first.

It wasn't likely that Mr. Weatherby would be at home, but perhaps his wife was and would be willing to talk to him.

To his surprise it was a man who clattered down the stairs and opened the inner door, a man almost as tall and rangy as Jake Fulford and wearing at the moment a rather distraught expression. "If you're another reporter—" he began.

"Nothing of the sort," said Richard, not much put out by the greeting. As it happened he had been occupied for some time in trying to concoct a tale that would explain his interest and had decided that there was nothing for it but the truth. Part of it at least. "I don't know if you've seen the paper today, or heard in any way, that a young friend of mine, Malcolm Stonor, has been arrested for the murder of the lady in the ground-floor flat."

"Heavens, man, I haven't time to read the papers," said Weatherby. "Or stand around gossiping, either." But he proved a moment later that he was not altogether without human curiosity. "Who's been arrested anyway?" he demanded.

Richard repeated himself. "A young friend of mine called Malcolm Stonor," he said. "He was a protégé of Mrs. Fielding's father, and mentioned in his will. He happens to have been visiting her last night, and that I suppose is what gave the police ideas as to his guilt."

"I've no interest in that," said Weatherby abruptly. "But if he knew her well he must have known her name and where she lived. Why did he come here, then?"

"Perhaps I could come in," Richard suggested, "then we can talk it over."

"Oh, if you must!" Weatherby retired ungraciously to allow him to enter. "I'm on the first floor," he remarked, "and I should be glad to hear your explanation."

"Mrs. Fielding gave him the address and said the flat belonged to a friend of hers," Richard told him, when they were settled upstairs in a room that was comfortable but untidy. A desk by the window with a typewriter and piles of paper seemed to suggest his host's occupation, and when Weatherby followed his eyes he gave a short laugh.

"My second novel, and I doubt if it will ever be finished," he said. "I left my job on the strength of the first one, but my savings are running out now."

"Oh, bad luck, but it looks as if you'd got a fair way along," said Richard encouragingly. In the circumstances the rather wild-eyed look became understandable, and he felt he owed the other man something for letting him in at all. And if the banker in him thought, if that's the case why set yourself up in one of the most expensive parts of town, he sternly suppressed the idea as being, for the moment, irrelevant.

"Well, I may decide to throw the whole thing in the fire, or I may read it over and find it's not so bad after all. We'll see. Meanwhile, perhaps you can explain to me why Mrs. Peabody, whom I've seen on and off for a couple of years now, should really be called something quite different."

"Geraldine Fielding. She lives in Hampstead and her husband, Maxwell, is an architect," said Richard. "As to what she was doing here calling herself Mavis Peabody, your guess is as good as mine."

"A love nest," said Weatherby, making Richard—forgetting he had used the phrase himself—hope that the other man's work was on the whole a little more original than that. "I don't see what else it could have been."

"There's only one name on the door, just the surname," said Richard. "I understand the flat was rented in the name of Mr. and Mrs. Hector Peabody, but how did you happen to know that?"

"Don't tell me you're suspecting me of having anything to do with the woman," said Weatherby, half alarmed, half amused. "She wasn't my type at all."

"No, no, nothing like that," Richard assured him. "I only wondered—"

"She mentioned him to me one day when we were chatting. My husband, Hector, something like that."

"How often did you see her, Mr. Weatherby?"

"Two or three times a week, I should say. At first we just passed the time of day, but later she'd stop for a word or two. Not that she ever told me a thing about herself; that was the only personal comment she ever made.''

''But you never saw the husband?''

''Neither hide nor hair of him.''

''And when you met her it was always late afternoon?''

''Yes, my habit is to work until four-thirty and then go for a walk. I generally finish up in a pub about opening time. It makes a change when you've been at the typewriter all day.''

''I see. So we must presume, perhaps, that Mr. Peabody left earlier.''

''Unless he stayed in all the time and never went out. Still it can't have been that. The police would have found him in the flat, wouldn't they? The whole thing is a mystery to me, and why they should suspect this young man you speak of—''

''Just because he happened to be there,'' said Richard, hoping against hope that that was true. ''Perhaps, Mr. Weatherby, you wouldn't mind telling me how you happened to find her on Sunday night.''

''Well, I don't mind at all. I don't suppose I'll get any more work done today anyway,'' said Weatherby rather ungraciously. ''We writers can't afford to be interrupted, you know.''

''I'm sorry,'' said Richard humbly. ''It really is important to me, though.''

''Yes, I suppose it must be. Well, I'd been to the pub as usual, and got home about eleven o'clock. The door of the Peabodys' flat was open, which was very unusual, and I thought perhaps they'd forgotten about it and I'd better remind them. So I knocked at the door but it just swung farther open, and then I called out but nobody answered. So I took a couple of steps inside thinking that I could make them hear better that way, and there were her feet sticking out from behind the sofa. To tell you the truth I don't much care to dwell on what I saw when I went farther into the room—it was distinctly messy. And do you know what I thought? It sounds ridiculous, but it came over me in a sort of wave. The room was full of anger, frustration, hatred...I don't quite know how to put it. Anyway, she was very dead.''

''Had you been in the flat before?''

''No, never. And if you're going to ask what it was like, I can only tell you that it looked as if a cyclone had hit it. If you ask me, somebody had been searching for something, but whether they found whatever it was or not I couldn't say.''

This was something Denby hadn't mentioned, though he had said—or had he only implied?—that there were no fingerprints besides Mrs. Fielding's own. ''Did the—the kind of disturbance that had been made,'' Richard asked, ''give you any clue as to what the person who did it might have been looking for?''

''Well, it couldn't have been anything big,'' said Weatherby. ''The sofa cushions and those of the one easy chair were pulled onto the floor; the writing desk near the window had all its drawers open and its contents spilled out. They'd even looked in the cupboard that had evidently been used as a bar. All the bottles were lying higgledy-piggledy on the floor, and the glasses from the shelf above had been pulled out carelessly so that I don't think one of them wasn't smashed. But I didn't penetrate any farther, you can imagine that. Do you think I might have discovered the murderer if I had done? It never occurred to me at the time.''

''If you telephoned the police from the Peabody flat and waited there for them to come, he wouldn't have had the chance to get away without being seen. No, I was forgetting, he might have gone by the window, I suppose, as it's on the ground floor.''

"He wouldn't have found it so easy. There's only one bedroom and to get out of that window he'd have to drop down into the area. The chances of somebody noticing him would have been pretty good. However, it doesn't apply; the Peabodys didn't have a phone, at least not in the sitting room. I had to come up here and use my own. And though the chap at the other end reacted pretty quickly it still took a moment or two to give the address and so on. Anyone could have got away within that time.''

"Well, I don't suppose it makes much difference either way," said Richard thoughtfully. "If the flat had been searched in such haste, your description of what had been done sounds as if you might have disturbed him. In that case it would be reasonable to suppose he made a getaway as soon as the coast was clear.''

"I don't much like the idea, but you're probably in the right of it.''

"Well, I must thank you for being so helpful," said Richard. "I'll leave you to get on with your work.''

"I don't suppose I'll write another word today," said Weatherby, but now he sounded quite cheerful about it. "There's a sort of fascination about this business, isn't there? And, by the way, do you realize you haven't even told me your name?''

"Richard Trenton.'' Richard had been realizing for some time that the other man had taken him remarkably on trust.

"And you're a friend of the man who's been arrested?''

"Yes, I think the police have got hold of the wrong man.''

"A lawyer perhaps? Your profession, I mean.''

"No, not a lawyer. I'm with the Northumberland and Wessex Bank.''

"And you're making your inquiries in their time," said Weatherby, glancing at his watch. Now that he was giving his mind to the problem he seemed to Richard to be uncomfortably acute. "However, I won't press you any further—confidential matters and all that. If the pubs were open I'd buy you a beer."

"I think it is I who should be playing host," said Richard, and also consulted his watch. "But I think, if you're going out now, you're going to have a pretty long walk before you get that drink you treat yourself to each evening."

"Well, I can think as I go," said Weatherby, who seemed quite cheerful now about his disturbed day. "Who knows, I may come up with a solution to the whole thing. You wouldn't like to give me a few more details, would you?" he added insinuatingly.

"I'm afraid I'm not at liberty. . . and anyway, I really know very little more than I told you," said Richard. "But if anything does occur to you, anything about the condition of the sitting room when you found Mrs. Fielding's body for instance, or if you remember seeing anyone who may have been Hector Peabody, and could describe him, I'd be awfully glad if you'd let me know." He produced a card and proffered it. "The home address would be best. I may not be in at the bank for a few days."

"So they *are* concerned with this Malcolm Stonor's fate!" said Weatherby, delighted by his own acumen. He crossed the room to put the card down on his working table. Richard entertained the gravest doubt whether he would ever find it again, but his host added, "Now I know where it is, it will be safe there," quite confidently.

"I suppose," said Richard, making for the door, "I shan't have such good luck upstairs as I've had here. Your neighbor—is it Mr. Marsh?—is likely to be out at work."

"It's Mr. and Mrs., and he will be out certainly, but I think you'll find her quite chatty." Weatherby followed him onto the landing and pulled the door to behind him. "Would you like me to come up and introduce you?"

"I think perhaps—" Richard began, but Weatherby interrupted him before he could formulate an excuse.

"Two's company, three's none," he said.

"I didn't quite mean that," said Richard, "only that sometimes people will talk more freely to one person than when there's a second man present."

"That's what I meant, too," said Weatherby. "Goodbye, Mr. Trenton, I hope we'll meet again. And I hope Mrs. Marsh is more informative than I was," he added, before he set off down the stairs at breakneck speed.

Mrs. Marsh, whose name turned out to be Janice, was not only in but eager for company, and after the first five minutes Richard was thinking that Weatherby might have warned him what he was in for. Unless the cryptic remark about two's company had been meant to do so. She was a good-looking woman in her early thirties, who obviously spent a good deal at the hairdresser's and on cosmetics, and she was dressed both comfortably and alluringly in a caftanlike garment covered with sprawling purple flowers. "A siren," said Richard, describing her later to Maggie, who only grinned at him in response and said, "That's so out of date, Richard, darling." Meanwhile, however, there was the problem of coping with his hostess, and Maggie much too far away to be of any help to him.

He explained his errand as briefly as he originally had done to Weatherby, and found her just as incurious. "But that's such a dreary subject," she said. "And anyway, there's nothing I can possibly tell you that the police don't know already."

"But I'm not the police," said Richard. "An interested friend of the man who's been accused of killing Mrs. Fielding, that's all."

"You mean Mavis Peabody," said Janice. "It was quite obvious what was going on, of course, and I find the whole affair rather sordid. Particularly where a middle-aged couple is concerned."

"You knew Mrs. Peabody, then?" said Richard, turning to the name she seemed to prefer.

"Not to say knew. I met her very, very occasionally, if I'd been out to lunch with Ted—that's my husband—and she arrived here at the same time as I came back."

"What time would that be?"

"Two o'clock, half past. But it only happened once or twice, as I've said."

"Were you asked to identify her?"

She grimaced at that. "The police showed me a photograph, that was quite nasty enough for me. And if you're wondering, it was certainly Mavis Peabody. She was a striking-looking woman, you know, in spite of her age, and of course the first time we met we introduced ourselves and I couldn't forget a name like that."

"You said, Mrs. Marsh, that it was quite obvious what was going on. Could you explain that to me?"

"Why, of course, very willingly. They weren't living there, just spending the afternoon occasionally. So it was obvious the Mr. and Mrs. bit must have been a fraud."

"It sounds like that, certainly."

"Well, I'm sure of it if you want to know, because Mary, who cleaned their place on Tuesdays, comes to me the other four weekday mornings. She never saw either of them; she was only there in the morning of course. There were drinks in the cupboard, and some cocktail snacks, but no food in the refrigerator, and as for clothes and toilet articles there

was just what they needed for that sort of thing,
not for living there permanently."

"I see. You're aware, aren't you, that Mrs. Peabody's real name was Geraldine Fielding?"

"Yes, the paper said so, but it's such a dreary subject," she said again. "Couldn't we talk about
something else now that you're here? I think I'll get
you a drink, Richard—you did say your name is
Richard, didn't you?—and then we can be really
comfortable and talk about ourselves."

"I won't have a drink, thank you, it's too early
for me," said Richard, feeling a prude as he did so.
"And I'm afraid you'd find me a very uninteresting
person if I were to try to tell you about myself."

She was pouring herself a drink, and another for
him in spite of his refusal, and her back was to him.
"Ted's a doctor," she said, "a heart specialist, but
one thing I refuse to do is live over the shop. What's
your line of business?"

"I'm a banker," said Richard, seeing no way to
avoid answering.

"That's fascinating," she said, though he could
have found another word for it. She came back
with the drinks and took the opportunity of seating
herself on the arm of his chair. "I've a sort of feeling you're a Scotch drinker. Is that right?"

"Yes, thank you." He cradled the glass between
his hands, not attempting to drink it.

"I see you as the manager of one of the biggest
branches in London," she said, her eyes half-closed
now as she invented his biography for him. "You
spend your whole day watching lords and ladies
crawl to you for overdrafts, and all the most important people on the stage, too, I shouldn't wonder.
What a marvelous feeling it must be to send them
away unsatisfied."

Richard laughed at that, and finding his glass too
full for comfort sipped a little to remedy this. "It

isn't quite like that," he told her. "You see, what nobody realizes is that banks really want to lend money—that's how they make their own living."

"Well, all I can say," said Janice, pouting a little, "is they don't behave that way. Ted always says they'll lend you money if you don't need it, not if you do."

"It must seem like that sometimes," said Richard, glad enough to have got on to what he felt was a safe topic. All the same he hadn't come here to talk about banking policy. "What I wish you'd tell me, Mrs. Marsh—"

"My name's Janice, I told you that."

"Yes, of course. What I wish you'd tell me is whether you ever saw Hector Peabody."

"Do you suppose that was really his name?"

"I haven't the faintest idea and it doesn't matter for the moment. The man who called himself Hector Peabody, if you prefer it."

"No, I never did, not to know it anyway. Of course I might have passed him in the street and been none the wiser, but I certainly never saw a man go into the ground-floor flat."

"Do you think Dr. Marsh might have done so?"

"No, I'm quite sure he never did. He's out all day, you know, and judging by what I saw of her they were only here in the afternoon. I was a bit curious sometimes. After all, it was rather a mystery. But Ted just said it's none of our business, and couldn't be bothered even to speculate about it."

"Then I won't trouble you any further," said Richard, looking round for a table on which to place his still almost full glass. Janice's arm was round his shoulders now, and he was going to find it difficult enough to get up without being encumbered by that, as well.

"But you haven't finished your Scotch," she protested. "I thought when we finished our business—

dull stuff, and I don't know what good it can do you—we could have a nice talk.''

"That would be delightful," said Richard insincerely, "but I'm afraid I haven't the time." He succeeded, by giving a convulsive wriggle, to get to his feet, spilling the whiskey down his trousers as he did so. "I'm really worried," he added, hoping that it would explain his disinclination for dalliance, "about this young friend of mine. And I want to see the estate agents who look after this property."

Janice subsided rather ungracefully into the chair. The pout was again very much in evidence. "Ted won't be home until six o'clock at least," she told him.

"And by that time the estate agents would be closed," said Richard, as good-humoredly as he could. It took him ten more minutes to make his escape gracefully, and he descended the stairs thinking unkind thoughts of Mr. Weatherby, who might at least have warned him.

. II

THE OFFICES of the estate agents concerned were not far distant, and here he varied his tactics a little. All the same, it took quite ten minutes, once they had realized he wasn't in the market for either a house or a flat, before he found himself in the office of the head of the firm, an elderly man who for some reason sported muttonchop whiskers and a drooping mustache. "Well, Mr. Trenton," he said, glancing at the card that had been carried in to him. "I hope your business won't take long. An inquiry on behalf of the bank, I understand."

"That's exactly right, and I daresay you won't think it a very important business," said Richard. "It's about the tenants of one of the flats you rent, who apparently took it under an assumed name."

"Ah, Mr. and Mrs. Peabody. Yes, we've had the police here about the murder. I don't quite see how it concerns your bank, though, Mr. Trenton."

"Not the murder of course," said Richard with less than honesty, "but the fact that the rent was apparently paid by an account at one of our branches, the Mayfair branch. Of course anyone can make a deposit and open an account, no proof of identity is required, but it was felt that some inquiry should be made, and whatever information was available gathered." He hoped that sounded specious enough and was relieved to see the other man nodding wisely.

"Yes, I understand," said the whiskered gentleman. Richard had been told his name and promptly forgotten it. "I have all the information at my fingertips, you know, because, as I told you, the police have been here already. The rent was certainly paid each month by a check on your Mayfair branch, signed by Mavis Peabody. I understand that that was not her real name, but there was never any question about the checks going through, so even if we had known there would have been nothing we could do about it."

"I presume, however, that you asked for references at the time the flat was originally taken."

"Of course we did. And this is rather odd, Mr. Trenton—" for the first time he showed some sign of humanity, settling himself in his chair as though prepared for a good gossip "—the name that was given to us was that of Maxwell Fielding, an architect whose office and home are in Hampstead. And now I understand that our Mrs. Peabody's real name was Geraldine Fielding, Mrs. Maxwell Fielding, in fact."

"That is odd," said Richard, for the moment completely taken aback. It was the last thing he had expected to hear. "Did you take up the reference?"

"Certainly we did. Our letter was sent to his home; that had been specified because it was a personal matter, not one that he would want to deal with at the office. I can't show you his letter in reply, because the police have it. But it was perfectly satisfactory in every way, and we had no hesitation in handing the keys over. I now understand that the premises were not used full-time, only occasionally, but that is hardly our affair."

"No, of course not. Did you never see either of the Peabodys?"

"The arrangements were made by telephone and then by letter. I suppose, come to think of it, we might have felt it strange that they had no interest in looking over the place. In fact one of the clerks mentioned it, but it occurred to me that they might have visited the previous tenants and had seen it that way. My senior clerk went round to Bruton Avenue by appointment to hand the keys over to Mrs. Peabody. That was the only direct contact any of us had with her."

It seemed worse than hopeless but, "Could I see him?" asked Richard.

"I'm afraid not. He died three months ago. It was a great shock to us all, because he was due to retire the following week."

"Oh, I'm sorry. Then I must thank you for your time and your courtesy," said Richard, "and leave you to whatever job it was I interrupted."

11

WHEN HE GOT BACK to Bread Court he had a little
while to wait before Jake was free to see him. "Ken
is back at the office again, but not really very fit,"
Fulford told him when he was at last shown into his
office, "and with my having to be absent so long
this morning at the magistrates' court it's put us all
behind."

"If I'm being a nuisance—" Richard began.

"Nonsense, you know I'm always glad to see you.
You're interested, and it will get matters clear in
my mind to talk about them."

"As a matter of fact," Richard admitted, "I'm
more interested than you think."

"What do you mean by that?"

"That the attitude at head office has completely
reversed itself. The general managers appear to be
quite willing to take my word for Malcolm's innocence, and—to introduce a cynical note—because if
he's acquitted he's a prospective client, they want
me to inquire into the matter. It's absolutely ridiculous, you know. In spite of what's happened in the
past it isn't my line at all. Those two occasions were
absolute accidents."

"I'm not so sure about that," said Jake. "I know I
for one would be glad of your help and suggestions."

"But you'll be putting a firm of inquiry agents onto the matter."

"That may be necessary, but they'll give me
facts, not opinions. From you I may get both."

"It's rather like being caught in cross fire," said Richard thoughtfully. "But as I'm under strict orders to carry on, I may as well accommodate you. You know I'm concerned about Malcolm's predicament and would certainly pass on anything I learned in any case."

"That's what I thought. I wonder," said Jake, "why you're so convinced of his innocence, after only one meeting with him."

Richard thought about that for a moment. "I suppose it must be my credulous nature," he said at last. "But from what Denby told me this was a violent crime, and not the sort of thing Malcolm Stonor could have brought himself to do under any circumstances. I thought you agreed with me."

"Yes, I do, but I know Malcolm better than you do. I was only wondering if, when you'd heard the rest of the evidence, your opinion would be quite so definite."

"Try me," Richard offered.

"Well, to begin with, the police theory. They think that Malcolm's talk with Geraldine Fielding didn't stop where he said it did. They think she told him that the will was in her possession, naming him among Jock Thorold's heirs, and that he was so infuriated, partly by the coldness with which the family had always treated him, and partly by the fact that she had been ready to swindle him, that he grabbed the nearest weapon and battered her to death."

"It's possible that she told him, of course, but the rest is just surmise," said Richard.

"Uncomfortably close to what might have happened," Fulford pointed out. "However Malcolm denied that when I spoke to him, and like you I'm inclined to believe him."

"You know, this didn't occur to me until I talked to the man who found the body this afternoon, but wouldn't there have been bloodstains? On the murderer, I mean.''

"The police have a theory about that, too. A perfectly logical explanation of what might have happened, in fact. Only not with Malcolm in the leading role.''

"What theory?''

"There was a dressing gown, a great voluminous thing that probably belonged to Mrs. Fielding. The maid identified it and said it always hung on the living-room door, along with an old-fashioned velvet smoking jacket. The implication being that both parties were in the habit of making themselves comfortable as soon as they entered the flat.''

"Yes, but—''

"The woman's gown, which Mrs. Fielding hadn't put on for her interview with Malcolm, was absolutely sodden with blood. If the killer turned to pick up the doorstop he could have snatched at it at the same time, wrapped himself in it, and dropped it where it was found when the deed was done. If whoever-he-was had any spots of blood on his face, say, or hands, that would be all, and quite easily disposed of. Malcolm admits he had a little time at home before Phil Lawson and the girl arrived.''

"There could have been traces on the washbasin.''

"There weren't, apparently, but the lack of them doesn't prove anything.''

"Nor in the bathroom at the apartment?'' Richard insisted.

"Nor there. What else is troubling you?''

"The finding of the will. Weatherby, whom I talked to this afternoon, says the flat had been searched—the sitting room that is, the only part of it he saw.''

"It had been searched very thoroughly, both rooms, kitchen and bathroom. And apparently by someone wearing gloves, as the murderer is said to have done.''

"Wait a bit. Wouldn't *that* imply premeditation? Nobody in their senses would be going about in gloves in weather like this.''

"That's a point.'' Jake made a note on the pad in front of him. ''And the will was found in the refrigerator under a tray of ice cubes. It had been securely taped in place there, so that anybody just pulling out the tray wouldn't be likely to notice it. Anyway, there it was, and if Malcolm had just found out about the legacy, but been doubtful of Geraldine's intentions, he might well have killed her and then carried out a frenzied search of the flat.''

"Yes, that puts him squarely in the picture as far as motive goes,'' said Richard. ''I've just thought of something, Jake. Even if he's convicted of Geraldine Fielding's murder, he'd still inherit under Thorold's will, wouldn't he?''

"One may not profit by a felony, but presumably none was committed when Jock Thorold died.''

"It's only just occurred to me. I'd been presuming. . . well, never mind that. Malcolm had motive and opportunity. What did the doctors say about the time of death?''

"They declined to commit themselves, which doesn't surprise me. She must have been alive to let Malcolm in at nine o'clock, and she was certainly dead when Weatherby found her at eleven, because he phoned the police almost immediately, he says. Somewhere between those limits, probably ten o'clock or soon after. Nothing a good counsel couldn't make hay with.''

"Well, then! Do those items amount to proof?''

"It isn't so much a matter of Malcolm having had the opportunity,'' said Jake carefully, ''as of his being the only one who could have done it. You see, there was the inevitable old lady in the window of the ground-floor flat opposite.''

"A witness,'' said Richard. "What had she to say?''

"She saw Malcolm arrive about nine-thirty. At least, she described him very clearly, and as he admits to being there there's no reason to doubt her word. She also saw him leave again, about half an hour later. She had seen him standing in the porch for a few minutes, but couldn't see who let him in. The trouble is, she swears nobody else entered that night. It was pointed out to her, of course, that Weatherby had come in about eleven, and she answered rather snappishly that she thought she was being asked about people who didn't live in the house.''

"An old lady, you said. Mightn't she have dropped off for a moment or two?''

"I shouldn't like the job of trying to get her to admit to that. She's an old lady, yes, but as sharp as a whip. The trouble is she's strengthened the case against Malcolm to the point where I think it may well hold.''

"In spite of the missing Mr. Peabody?''

"In spite of that. The defense will make what play we can, of course, with the fact that Mrs. Fielding must have had a lover, but that's a far way from proving who he was or that he killed her.''

"He'd have a key. Couldn't he have arrived without this old lady of yours having seen him?''

"That can be suggested, too, but I doubt if the jury would believe it in face of her certainty.''

"Then what about Weatherby?''

"What about him?''

"He could have let himself into the house, found her door open, as he says, or knocked and been admitted, and then killed her.''

Jake looked at him with a half-smile playing

round his lips. "I believe you told me that lad of
yours is always full of theories," he remarked.
"That sounded very much like something he might
have come up with."

"It's a possibility," said Richard stubbornly.

"Well, I suppose strictly speaking it is, but why on
earth should he have done such a thing?"

"Perhaps when Peabody wasn't there he was
having an affair with Geraldine himself. A full-
blooded crime of passion," said Richard, "and I
hope to goodness that isn't something Ricky is going
to suggest to me just yet. Seriously, Jake—"

"You've been talking to Weatherby this afternoon. Did he strike you as a possible killer?"

"No, I have to say he didn't. He's a writer, and
when I arrived he had straws in his hair about being interrupted. But afterward he was pleasant
enough, and I'd say he had a sense of humor. But I
suppose some murderers do have a sense of humor,
don't they?"

"I daresay they do. There are three flats in that
house, aren't there? What about the top floor?"

"That's occupied by a Dr. and Mrs. Marsh. He
wasn't in, and she maintains he's never seen either
of their ground-floor neighbors. She was full of gossip she'd got from her maid, who looks after their
flat as well as the one the Peabodys occupied. What
she had to say coincided with what Denby told me:
there were no signs of permanent occupancy. And
if you're going to suggest that I go back there again
with any more questions, even if the good doctor is
present, I can tell you the answer is no."

Jake grinned again. "Like that, was it?"

"Exactly like that. Of course, either of them
could have come down and committed the murder
without being seen by the old lady across the street,
between the time Malcolm left and the time Weatherby came home. But I can't for the life of me see

any motive; they didn't even know who she really
was.''

''Did you learn anything else in the course of your
inquiries this afternoon?''

''Yes, I did as a matter of fact. Something rather
odd. I went round to see the estate agents who were
responsible for the letting.''

''The checks were signed Mavis Peabody in Geraldine Fielding's writing,'' said Jake, ''but I gather
nobody there had ever seen either of them, except
the chief clerk, who has since died.''

''That's correct enough, but there was something
else that you may not have heard. I told them the
bank wanted an inquiry made because an account
had been opened in false names at the Mayfair
branch. Then I asked about references, because I
think they're rather a stuffy sort of firm, and even
with the first quarter's rent paid in advance I
thought they'd be almost sure to ask for them.''

''And had they?''

''They had, and been given Mr. Maxwell Fielding's name,'' said Richard impressively. ''They
were asked to write to him at his home address as it
was a personal matter. The chap I talked to couldn't
show me his reply, because the police have it. Presumably they're comparing signatures.''

''That sounds like a put-up job of some sort,'' said
Jake, genuinely puzzled now. ''But if it was the two
Fieldings who rented the flat, why on earth should
they call themselves Peabody?''

''I'm not sure it was,'' said Richard. ''I've had a
bit of time to think it over, you see. The request
that the letter should be sent home is the first clue.
Geraldine could have intercepted it and sent the
reply herself. Obviously it wouldn't be difficult to
get hold of some of her husband's official letterhead.''

''That's possible, of course. In fact, if Peabody

was her lover that's the only way it could have been.''

"My instructions from the bank are to find him," said Richard.

"That's all very well, but how do you mean to set about it?"

"I'm going to start by making an assumption. You may or may not agree with me, Jake, but I've got to have a starting point somewhere."

"What is this assumption, then?" said Fulford cautiously.

"That Peabody was one of the family, one of her sisters' husbands in fact."

"How do you make that out?"

"That will turned up from somewhere. If one of them wanted it secreted for some reason, don't you think that would have been a good place? Nobody knew who the Peabodys really were."

"It's still a pretty big assumption."

"I'm quite aware of that, but you do see what I mean about having a starting place, don't you?"

"Yes, I see that all right. Are you further supposing that Geraldine came across the will by accident and that when the man concerned found out he killed her?"

"That's one possibility. The other is that she knew about it all the time, and it was only my remarks that Sunday afternoon that made her realize for the first time that perhaps it was not fair to keep Malcolm Stonor from his inheritance. Either way the result might have been the same, and I prefer the first idea, of course, because otherwise it makes me feel responsible."

"Now you're going much too fast, Richard. Even if your guess is correct there's no question of responsibility. But all that raises a number of questions, you know, rather more than it answers in fact."

"I'm aware of that." Richard glanced at his
watch. "Think of some answers for me by tomorrow, there's a good chap," he suggested. "Meanwhile I'll do my best to talk to the Lawsons and the
Bennetts again, and to the widower, of course. I'm
not looking forward to that. But I don't think
there's anything more we can usefully say at the
moment."

Jake Fulford agreed to that and accompanied his
friend down to the street. "I shall be seeing Malcolm again tomorrow morning," he said, and then
laughed. "Do you know you've never even asked
me whether he was committed for trial?"

"I assumed that if he hadn't been you'd have told
me," said Richard. "There's one question you
might ask him, though, if you don't mind."

"What's that?"

"The relationships between the various family
members. I know they all kept him at a distance,
but he must have seen something of them and perhaps he can give us a clue."

"I'll do that," Jake promised, and to Richard's
surprise shook his hand before they parted.

II

THAT EVENING Ricky had come home hungry and
had been regaled with the highest of high teas before his father arrived. He was helping his mother
to clear away when he heard Richard's key in the
lock and quickly abandoned this filial task in favor
of the more congenial one of asking questions.
"Daddy's here," he announced unnecessarily to
Maggie, as he rushed out into the hall. "Have you
found out who did it, daddy?" he demanded.

"I told you last night—"

"Yes, but things have changed since then. I know
you came home to lunch because there were two

glasses on the draining board and two plates."
("Heaven help me if I ever want to entertain the
milkman," said Maggie later.) "And now you're
home later than you usually are. You changed your
mind and decided it was only fair to help Chief Inspector Denby after all," said Ricky accusingly.

"Denby doesn't want my help, which is about the
only thing there is to be thankful for," he added in
a sort of aside to Maggie. "I'm late, Ricky, because
I've been talking to Mr. Fulford and I was going to
do that anyway."

"I read all about it in the paper this morning,"
said Ricky importantly, leading the way into the living room. Maggie glanced helplessly at her husband,
shrugged slightly and followed him. By the time
Richard went in, too, she was already pouring him a
whiskey, which reminded him uncomfortably of
Mrs. Marsh's ministrations. However, he accepted it
without comment and went to his usual chair.

"Then you know it all, Ricky. As much as I do certainly."

"I don't suppose that's true," said Ricky. He spoke
more in sorrow than in anger, well used to the ways
of grown-ups and to their habit of avoiding his questions. "This man you like, daddy, the one the police
say did it, has he no imagination at all?"

"Imagination?" said Richard, immediately divert-
ed. "I'd say actually he's a rather solid sort of chap,
but he's shown a good deal of sensitivity one way
and another toward other people's feelings, so I
don't think you could put him down as being un-
imaginative."

"There, you see! He couldn't have done anything
so—so commonplace," said Ricky, using the word
with pride, "as to kill that lady with a blunt instrument. It's the oldest trick in the world."

"That's a point in his favor certainly," said Richard, trying to keep a smile out of his voice.

Maggie, who had been sitting quietly sipping her sherry, intervened now. "Who's going to defend him, Richard?" she asked.

"I don't know who his counsel will be, but Jake is preparing the brief, of course," said Richard. "There are one or two unexplained things about it, but the most important fact is what I learned from Jake just now. An old lady opposite, who spends her days sitting in the window, swears nobody went into the house in Bruton Avenue except Malcolm Stonor until the other man went in, the one who lives there, and discovered Mrs. Fielding."

"His name was Weatherby," said Ricky, who had obviously made good use of his time studying the newspaper.

"That's right. I suggested to Jake that he might have done it himself," said Richard, smiling from his son to his wife, "but I don't think he liked the idea. In fact, Ricky, he said it's just the sort of thing you might have suggested yourself."

"Nothing so ordinary," said Ricky, on his dignity. "Though, of course, anyone in the house already might have done it."

"We went into all that," Richard assured him, "and it seems very unlikely."

"Well, there are two things I don't understand, daddy."

"Only two?" asked Richard quizzically.

"Two main things," Ricky conceded. "It said in the paper that Mr. and Mrs. Fielding had their home in Hampstead. So I don't see why they wanted another place where they called themselves Peabody."

"I'm afraid I don't understand that, either," said Richard seriously, thinking as he spoke that there were, after all, certain things to be thankful for.

"I expect they just wanted somewhere where they could be quite alone, away from the children," said Ricky. "Don't you ever wish you two could get away alone together, without me?"

"Of course we don't, Ricky, darling," said Maggie warmly, "and—"

"We couldn't afford it in any case," said Richard almost simultaneously, smiling at his son. Ricky could be relied on to distinguish a teasing remark from a serious one.

"Well, if I were different," said Ricky, "I think you might want to get away. But the other question, daddy, is something I don't understand at all. What is a hol-holograph will?"

"Oh, one written in the testator's own hand. Haven't you come across one in all the reading you do, Ricky?"

"No, I don't think so. Of course I know all about witnesses, and that they have to be present together at the same time that the will is signed . . . something like that. But that was a new one to me."

"Well, there are rules about a holograph will, too, but I don't think it needs any witnesses. The thing is, it would be invalidated if you wrote it on a sheet of letterhead, for instance, and allowed the printed address there to stand as part of the whole. And, of course, people quite easily make mistakes. It's really better to go to a lawyer, but Mr. Fulford says this one is quite in order."

"Why *didn't* Mr. Thorold go to a lawyer?" said Ricky consideringly. "After all, he had one in the family."

Richard had rapidly come to the conclusion that his son had learned the newspaper report by heart. "Yes, his son-in-law," he agreed. "But I don't know the answer to that, either."

"There are an awful lot of things you don't know," said Ricky frankly. He had been lying on his stomach on the hearth rug before the empty grate, but now he jumped to his feet. "I'd like to paint for an hour before I go to bed, mummy. Will I be in the way in the kitchen?"

"Not a bit of it, Ricky. You might turn the oven on for me though, about 250. There's a casserole ready inside," she added to Richard, as the boy left the room. "Why do you think old Mr. Thorold didn't use Mr. Lawson to make his will?"

"The family was thoroughly opposed to his doing anything for Malcolm Stonor. I ought to say I don't think Lawson was himself, but-it would have been bound to get as far as Eleanor Lawson at least, and I think old Jock didn't want any unpleasant reaction. So he made it himself and was clever enough to do it properly. The mystery is, what happened to it after that?"

"As Geraldine Fielding seems to have disliked Malcolm quite as much as her sisters did, I can't imagine why he gave it into her keeping," said Maggie. "I'm glad that Ricky took it for granted it was her husband she had been sharing the Mayfair flat with, aren't you, Richard?"

"Yes, I thought that myself, but if he goes on reading at the rate he does he won't retain his innocence on that sort of a point much longer," he pointed out.

Maggie sighed her agreement and then said, "Now that we're alone, tell me about your day, Richard, darling."

So Richard did, making a good story about his encounter with Janice Marsh. Maggie was laughing when he finished. "But what does it all mean?" she asked.

"I don't know, but I formed. . .I think you might call it a working hypothesis," said Richard, "if that doesn't sound too grand."

"I can't think of any other way of putting it," said Maggie, "but what is it?"

"That Hector Peabody must be one of Jock Thorold's sons-in-law. Otherwise I don't see how the will comes into it, and it's obvious that it does somewhere."

"You mean that Geraldine Fielding was having an affaire with one of her own sisters' husbands?"

"It's not altogether unknown. Propinquity has a lot to answer for. It's only a starting point, but I have to make certain assumptions or I'll never get anywhere at all."

"I suppose in that case Maxwell Fielding is out of it altogether."

"No, I don't think so."

"You're not telling me there's something in Ricky's suggestion," said Maggie, amused.

"Not exactly as he worded it. Though there are times, my dearest love, when being alone together seems the most desirable state in the world." Maggie raised her glass to him in a mock salute. "But I was thinking there might be something not quite normal in their relationship, so that getting away alone together where no one even knew their real names might seem desirable to them."

"A sort of perversion," said Maggie, wrinkling her nose over the word. "Or is that too strong a way of putting it?"

"I'm not a psychologist, but I don't think so," said Richard. "I think there may be people who get a kick out of a thing like that. A secret life that nobody else dreamed of."

"So Mr. Fielding stays on your list. What about the others?"

"I suppose Philip Lawson is the most likely. Suppose Jock Thorold decided to make his will and then suffered from doubts when he had done so in case it wouldn't stand up. He might have sworn Philip Lawson to secrecy and consulted him about it, perhaps even left the thing in his possession."

"But you thought he made a holograph will because he didn't want Mr. Lawson to know."

"Yes, I'm just postulating that he may have changed his mind. And though I think Lawson feels himself bound now to abide by his wife's and sisters-in-law's wishes—or did when it was a question of taking out letters of administration—I think he might quite well have accepted a fait accompli as being Jock Thorold's right."

"In that case, why hide it? Why all that show of sympathy for Malcolm?"

"I don't know. I'm only thinking aloud," said Richard in a depressed way.

"There's another son-in-law," said Maggie.

"Yes, Wilfred Bennett. He's a builder and contractor, works closely with Maxwell Fielding, or did I tell you about that before? The trouble there is that I can't see any reason why Jock Thorold should have told him about the will; he wouldn't be in a position to advise him as to its validity. And he was very vehement against anything being done at all for Malcolm Stonor, so Jock could hardly have expected him to sympathize with what he was doing."

"What about the younger generation, Jock's grandchildren?" said Maggie slowly.

"I think the Fieldings' eldest is twenty, but the whole lot of them are away either at school or university. The Bennetts' daughter is only a child. I'm not sure of her age, I got the impression of something around eight."

"You haven't mentioned Phil Lawson," said Maggie.

"Well, he certainly wasn't Peabody, but in any case he was with Joanna, and then here. I'm working on the assumption that the murderer was probably in the bedroom while Geraldine was talking to Malcolm, in spite of his impression to the contrary, and that perhaps he was still there when Weatherby discovered the body. Weatherby had to go upstairs to phone, so Peabody—whoever he is—could have made his escape then.''

"Yes, I understand. You don't think Malcolm was framed?''

"In this case, no. I think his being there, and the evidence against him, was sheer accident. So if you're thinking, Maggie, that Phil Lawson might have wanted his rival out of the way, I believe you're stretching things a little.''

"Yes, I suppose I am. What are you going to do now, Richard? I gather from what you told me of your talk with Mr. Jarvis that the general managers have forgiven you for what you did over the weekend.''

"Yes, I think they have,'' said Richard rather ruefully. "But I'm afraid my continuing to bask in the sunshine of their pleasure depends rather on the outcome of these inquiries. The queer thing is that Jake is almost as bad as Ricky—he wants my help.''

"Well, I don't wonder at that,'' said Maggie stoutly.

"But there's nothing I can do—don't you see?—if I'm wrong about the family. If Peabody isn't one of the people we've mentioned, I've no facilities for tracking him down.''

"Then you must persuade Chief Inspector Denby to do it.''

"There's not a hope of that. As far as the police are concerned the case is closed, except for gathering any further evidence against Malcolm, which I expect they will do assiduously enough.''

"Then you'll talk to the family again?''

"Certainly I will, as quickly as I can manage it.''
Before he could say anything else Ricky had burst into the room.

"I'm going to bed,'' he announced. "And I've put everything away very carefully, mummy,'' he added virtuously. But he turned in the doorway to give his father one last, reproachful look. "I expect you've been talking about it all the time I've been gone, daddy," he said. "It's all very simple really, and I think if you tell Chief Inspector Denby this you won't have to bother about it anymore. It's bound to have been the least likely person."

As the door closed behind him Richard and Maggie exchanged looks and both began to laugh. "It isn't funny," said Richard after a moment, "but I should like to see Denby's face if I told him that."

III

RICKY HAD CERTAINLY DONE some mopping up, but there were still signs on Maggie's scrubbed tabletop where some indigo blue had been spilled. "Which explains why he took himself to bed," said Maggie resignedly, looking for her scrubbing brush. "I was afraid he might be ill."

By the time they had got things back to normal again the casserole was bubbling merrily. They had their dinner and cleared away, but Richard had no sooner settled down in the living room with Jane's latest epistle to read than the doorbell rang. "Are we expecting anyone?" he asked, looking across at his wife.

Maggie took off her spectacles, which he always said affectionately gave her an owllike look, and laid down the evening paper beside her. "Not that I know of," she said, the anxiety back in her voice again, as was so often her reaction to the unexpected. Their friends didn't often call without warning; they regarded the Trentons' choice of living in the City of London too eccentric for that, and too out of the way. "I'll see who it is if you like."

Richard went back to Jane's letter again. Until the Easter holidays she had written in a large round hand, which he found quite easy to decipher, but the last time she was home she had informed him rather self-importantly that she was old enough now to develop a style of her own. Ever since, her writing had been almost illegible. He was struggling with a word that might equally be "match" or "midterm" when he became aware that Maggie's voice in the hall had been joined by a deeper, rumbling one. "Not you again, Chief Inspector!" he said, laying the letter aside as Denby followed Maggie into the room.

This time the detective was alone. He stood surveying Richard for a moment, and then said without any attempt at a formal greeting—but then Richard's greeting had not been exactly a model of politeness, either—"You'll never learn, will you, Mr. Trenton?" He turned slightly then to address Maggie directly. "Mrs. Trenton, I wonder if you'd excuse us for a moment. There's something I want to say to your husband."

Maggie was undoubtedly flustered, and glanced at Richard before she replied. "Of course you can talk alone if you like, Mr. Denby," she said, "but I hope you won't keep him long. He's had a long, tiring day."

With that she left them. Denby's look as he turned to Richard was definitely sardonic. "Am I supposed to sympathize with you about that?" he wondered.

"I don't need your sympathy. But I should like to know exactly why you're here," said Richard.

Denby didn't reply immediately. He seemed to be thinking out the best way of expressing himself. "I suppose you might say I'm here to warn you, Mr. Trenton," he said then. "I've had occasion to speak to you before about the possible ill effects of interference, and we both know what your completely unauthorized inquiries over the weekend led to."

"You may know," said Richard, "but I don't. Unless you're accusing me of having provided a motive for someone to kill Geraldine Fielding."

"That was in my mind," said Denby. "You put the cat among the pigeons," he added, with a flight of fancy of which Richard would not have believed him capable, "and one of them got killed."

"That takes a little sorting out. To round off your metaphor we'd have to say that one pigeon killed another, which I don't think very often happens. You're not telling me there's been another murder?" he said with sudden anxiety.

"Isn't one sufficient?"

"Quite sufficient," said Richard, recovering himself. "Though it might at least have made you wonder whether you'd been mistaken in making an arrest so quickly. But if that isn't the case, I suppose you've heard somehow that in spite of what I said last night I'm continuing my inquiries. What I told you was true, when I said it, but circumstances have changed since then."

"You mean, perhaps, that your friend Mr. Fulford has persuaded you—"

"Nothing of the sort, though he doesn't seem to regard my activities with quite such horror as you do. My superiors at the bank—" He didn't attempt to complete the sentence but added, more persuasively, "It's no good, Chief Inspector, I'm bound to consider their wishes before yours. And where a good customer is concerned, our—our solicitude for his welfare knows no bounds."

"I suppose I should say I'm relieved to hear it," said Denby dryly. "Yes, I did hear you'd been visiting the tenants in the Mayfair house, and the estate agent, as well. I hope you found your visits illuminating."

"Not particularly. I'm quite sure I learned nothing you didn't already know, Chief Inspector, if

that's what you want to find out. But you can tell
me one thing. Who signed the reference for Mr.
and Mrs. Hector Peabody in Maxwell Fielding's
name?"

"Can you give me one good reason why I should
answer that question?"

"None, except that perhaps I might give you a tip
in return," said Richard. Suddenly, in spite of the
chief inspector's obvious antagonism, he found his
spirits soaring and felt himself completely in command of the situation.

"Very well," said Denby, though his look was
skeptical. "As you surmise, the letter was signed
Maxwell Fielding, but our experts tell us it was Mrs.
Fielding's handwriting."

"I thought that might be the case. Tell me, Chief
Inspector, who do *you* think Hector Peabody is?"

"He might be anybody in London, anybody in the
country for that matter."

"Or he might have come over on an excursion
from the continent," said Richard. "Doesn't his existence create any difficulties in your mind? About
Malcolm Stonor's guilt or innocence, I mean."

"If it weren't for the finding of the will—"

"Ah, yes, there I agree with you. That does bring
the members of the family rather to the center of
the stage, doesn't it?"

"So I suppose the next series of interviews you
conduct will be with them."

"If they will consent to see me, yes."

"May I point out to you that it was only Stonor
who would benefit by the will being found? The
three daughters would have inherited one third of
the estate each instead of a quarter, if Jock Thorold
had died intestate."

"Someone searched the Mayfair flat in a rather
frantic attempt to find the will," Richard pointed
out.

"That might equally have been to ensure that it was discovered as to destroy it. It's no use, Mr. Trenton, you're letting your sympathies run away with you, and these inquiries of yours are quite unjustified. I ought to warn you that there are quite serious penalties for interfering with the police, and for a man in your position the consequences might be even more serious."

"I'm not proposing to brawl with you, Chief Inspector."

"No, I don't suppose you are." Denby's smile was rather grim. "I wasn't referring to anything physical, but the Act covers anything that makes it more difficult for the police to carry out their duties. Ask your friend Mr. Fulford about it if you don't believe me."

"I believe you all right, but I don't see how my actions can interfere with you in any way. Or . . . are your inquiries continuing?"

"There are still questions to which the director of public prosecutions requires an answer."

"I'm sure there are. Well, you've delivered your warning, Chief Inspector, and I'm sorry to tell you it fell on deaf ears. Is there anything else?"

"You said, if I remember your words aright, that you might give me a tip in return for the information you asked of me."

"Oh, yes." Richard smiled and allowed a moment to pass before he attempted to answer. "It's just something that my young son said to me on his way to bed."

"I've met the boy," said Denby. "A bright lad, I'll grant you that, but I decline to believe he knows anything about this matter."

"No, he doesn't, but I think you might take his advice all the same. He said that the thing to do was to look for the most unlikely person—they were always guilty," said Richard, and had the pleasure of seeing, after all, the detective's reaction to this gratuitous piece of wisdom.

Denby regarded him for a long moment in silence, then he turned on his heel and left the flat, passing Maggie in the hallway without a word.

"And what was all that about?" she said blankly.

"Come back in here," Richard invited. "Nothing at all to worry about, Maggie. On the question of making inquiries I'm damned if I do and I'm damned if I don't, it seems. But I'm just beginning to realize that I've been regarding this matter in a purely selfish light. Malcolm Stonor, if he is indeed innocent, has his point of view, as well, and is entitled to his freedom."

"That means. . . Richard, darling, does that mean you've got an idea?"

"It came to me while I was talking to Denby," he admitted, "but it's far too vague to tell you about it. I will when I can, I promise, even if I'm wrong," he added, smiling at her.

"You're going to talk to all those people again tomorrow," said Maggie questioningly. "Can Mr. Denby do anything to stop you?"

"Not a thing. Oh, there's some Act he quoted to me about obstructing the police, but there's absolutely no question that any action could be taken on that. What worries me more is that he said if I'd never started this business in the first place Geraldine Fielding might still be alive. That can't be true, can it, Maggie?"

"Only, I suppose, if Malcolm Stonor is really guilty," said Maggie slowly. "Then the fact that you and Mr. Fulford took his part might have put ideas into his head. I mean, perhaps the meeting with Mrs. Fielding was at his suggestion, not hers."

"That couldn't be so, he wouldn't have known where to go. Remember she had the flat under a false name."

"Yes, but she might have agreed to see him and told him to meet her there just as he said she did. But I don't believe it for a moment," she added firmly. "I'm quite sure he's as innocent as you think."

"Denby said I was letting my sympathies run away with me," said Richard. "Do you think that's what I'm doing?"

"Look at it this way," said Maggie, immediately regretting that she had spoken what was no more than a stray thought aloud. "Supposing Malcolm came to you for a loan at the bank, what would you say to him?"

"That would depend."

"Oh, yes, I know, on whether he had any prospect of repaying it, of course. But character comes into it, too," she insisted. "What judgment would you have made of him under those circumstances?"

"All things being equal he'd have got the loan," said Richard. "But I'm out of my depth, Maggie, way out of my depth. And I just wish I was in a position to take Denby's advice."

12

A PHONE CALL to Philip Lawson's office the following morning revealed that he had a heavy schedule that day, but after a little argument he promised to find ten minutes if Richard would be there at ten o'clock. So again there was a chance for a quiet moment with Maggie after Ricky had gone to school, though Richard's restlessness drove him to leave the flat earlier than he need have done, and he had to cool his heels for quite a quarter of an hour waiting for Lawson to be free.

Philip greeted him politely enough, but allowed his surprise at the visit to be apparent. "I thought we'd seen the last of you, Mr. Trenton," he said frankly when they were both seated. "Though it seems you were right in what you told us about Jock's intentions. Have you come to say, I told you so?"

"Nothing like that." Richard had spent a restless night thinking over the difficulties of the task he had set himself and wondering how best to succeed. Also during that time his concern for Malcolm Stonor had grown, so that perhaps it was natural that he blurted out what was uppermost in his mind. "I'm worried about the possibility of a miscarriage of justice," he said.

That brought Lawson up short, so that he thought for a moment before he spoke again. "I should be concerned, too, if I thought one had taken place," he said. "But it seems obvious that Malcolm resented having no share in the estate, and personally I feel some sympathy for him about that. If Geraldine told him that a will in fact existed—''

''Yes, I know that's the theory the police are going on, but there are difficulties, don't you see that, Mr. Lawson? Where had the will been all this time, and how did Mrs. Fielding get hold of it?''

''I can't help you there. And I can't really see why you're concerning yourself any further with Malcolm's affairs. After all, think how things stand now. If he's convicted he'll serve nine years, perhaps ten. Meanwhile our friend Mr. Blake will have looked after his affairs. He'll be a wealthy man when he comes out, and still young.''

''Have you thought what those years in prison might do to him?''

''Yes, of course I have. I know if it was Phil. . . but perhaps if he has a clever counsel it may not even be as long as that, Mr. Trenton. After all, I think diminished responsibility might be a good plea when all the facts are known.''

''That's what you would advise if you were acting for him? That he should plead guilty and rely on the court feeling some sympathy for his emotions?''

''I think it's good advice,'' said Lawson, and glanced at his watch. ''Mr. Trenton—''

''My ten minutes aren't up yet,'' said Richard quickly. ''You're ignoring, I think, the existence of Hector Peabody. What did you think when you heard of your sister-in-law's death, where she was found and the name she had been known by there?''

''I was completely dumbfounded.'' For the first time Philip Lawson seemed to be speaking with complete spontaneity. ''If you'd known Geraldine. . . you must have gathered for yourself that what worried her about letting Malcolm share the estate was the suggestion that he might have been

Jock Thorold's natural son. It shocked her tremendously."

"I seem to have said this before," said Richard, "but people can follow a course of action themselves that they would condemn in their parents, illogical though that may be."

"Yes, I know. I've told myself that."

"The police must have asked you whether you had any idea who Hector Peabody might be."

"Have you looked in the phone book?" asked Lawson dryly.

"He isn't—never was—living in the Mayfair flat."

"That wasn't what I meant. I suppose you're going to tell me that as an illicit relationship seems to have been involved the man was unlikely to be using his own name."

"That's exactly what I think. So I ask you again, Mr. Lawson, have you any idea who Peabody might have been?"

"I know most of Max and Gerry's friends, of course, living so near and Eleanor being so close to her sisters. And I can't imagine in any circumstances at all that she could have been romantically entangled with any of them."

"Her relationship with her husband—" Richard began.

"Mr. Trenton! I think," said Philip, "that's going rather beyond the bounds of good taste."

"Yes, I'm sure it is. But you might say that to be charged with a murder you didn't commit wasn't very good taste, either," said Richard. "That's what's worrying me."

"Do you really think Malcolm might be innocent?"

"Yes, I do."

"Why?"

"Because his guilt leaves too many things unexplained, for one thing. The other is the boy's character. From what you knew of him, Mr. Lawson, would you think he could have lost his temper in that way?''

"I wouldn't think it of anybody," said Lawson unhappily. "Oh, well, ask your questions. I'll do my best to answer them. Though I can't see how it can help you."

"I asked, if you remember, about Mrs. Fielding's relationship with her husband."

"I may as well be honest with you, I could never see what she saw in him. He's a wishy-washy sort of fellow," said Philip, who having put his inhibitions aside seemed to have done so wholeheartedly. "But that's the sort of chap—have you noticed?—who always has a large family. I always thought they got on well enough together."

"I have three children myself," said Richard, and smiled at his host.

"My dear fellow, I didn't mean—"

"I know you didn't, and I know what you mean about the pale young curate type. The Mayfair flat seems to have been in use for a little over two years, and mainly to have been used in the afternoons. Can you tell me anything about Mrs. Fielding's absences from home?"

"You'd have to ask Eleanor about that...and heaven help you if you do," said Philip frankly. He eyed Richard closely for a moment. "That's what you mean to do, isn't it? See us all again, one after the other."

"Yes, that's exactly what I mean to do," said Richard.

"You're thinking that one of us—"

"Not necessarily." There were times, Richard thought, when it wasn't advisable to be completely honest. "Have you any objections to my talking to Mrs. Lawson?"

Philip gave a sudden bark of laughter. "No objection at all, if you don't mind taking your life in your hands," he said.

"I don't like to intrude at a time like this, but—"

"Nonsense, you've every intention of doing so. Anyway, it may take her mind off things. That could only be to the good." He was getting to his feet as he spoke, and again his watch was in evidence. "I really must ask you to go now, Mr. Trenton," he said. "I did warn you, if you remember, that I could only spare you a few minutes."

"Why didn't Jock Thorold ask you to make his will?" Richard asked, getting up in his turn.

"Oh, that's easy. My wife and her sisters were all dead against doing anything for Malcolm. I suppose he didn't want the fact that he was going against their wishes to get back to them. As a matter of fact I'd have respected his confidence, but it seems he felt he couldn't trust me."

"You're sure he didn't change his mind about that?"

"Quite sure," said Lawson, for the first time looking on the verge of losing his temper.

"I was just wondering," said Richard vaguely, "how the will came to be in Mrs. Fielding's possession. But perhaps, as you say, one of her sisters will know more about her affairs than you do."

Lawson's parting was a little cooler than his reception had been. Richard found a convenient pay phone in the lobby of the building in which Philip Lawson's office was situated and rang the number of the Hampstead house.

II

IT WAS PHIL LAWSON who answered his call. "Yes, mother's in," he said doubtfully. "Do you want to see her, Mr. Trenton? She's pretty cut up, you know."

"I'm sure she must be. All the same, if it's at all possible...." Richard let the sentence trail there and was rewarded for his vagueness when Phil answered him.

"Well, I don't think I'd better ask her," he said. "But come along, she's certainly at home. In fact, today would probably be the best time. The inquest is tomorrow and she won't be in the mood to see anybody after that. And then with any luck Uncle Max will be able to arrange the funeral."

"I'd like to talk to you, too, Phil."

"Well, my time is yours. I'm not going anywhere today. Come along right away," he added more encouragingly.

Eleanor Lawson might indeed have been upset by her sister's death, as Phil had asserted, but when her son showed Richard into the drawing room—again he had been the one who had opened the front door—she showed very little sign of it. She had been standing by the window, and when she turned her face was in the shadow, but her voice was quite steady. "Phil says I should see you, Mr. Trenton. I think he has an idea it may distract me from my grief. But I may as well be honest with you, I see no reason at all for this intrusion at such a time."

"If you will allow me to express my sympathy for your loss—" Richard began, but wasn't allowed to finish. She swept across the room toward him and seated herself regally.

"I can only guess at your errand," she said. "When you visited us before you were very concerned with the welfare of the young man, Malcolm Stonor. Are you now concerned on his behalf, also, because if that is the case, all I can say is that an expression of sorrow at my sister's death comes very badly from a friend of her murderer."

"Come now, mother," said Phil, "you know you

mustn't prejudge the issue. And the fact is you're as curious as I am to know what Mr. Trenton wants, so don't pretend you aren't.''

''That will do, Phil. If you wish to stay you'd better sit down, and Mr. Trenton, too. I don't like people looming over me.''

They both seated themselves obediently. Phil sprawled in his chair, which Richard took in some way to be an act of defiance, though he would have been hard put to it to explain exactly what he meant by that. He himself found it quite impossible to relax, and chose a straight-backed chair so that the fact wouldn't be too obvious.

''You're quite right in one way, Mrs. Lawson. I like Malcolm and find it hard to believe—''

Again he wasn't allowed to complete the sentence. ''And he is now a very wealthy young man,'' said Eleanor dryly.

''If I must be honest, I think that is my employers' concern,'' Richard admitted. ''If it hadn't been for their insistence I might not be bothering you again. On the other hand, I think perhaps I might. There isn't only my own conviction that Malcolm would be very unlikely to do such a thing, but the theory of his guilt leaves a great many things unexplained.''

''You'd better tell us what you mean by that, Mr. Trenton.''

''How the will came to be in Mrs. Fielding's possession, for instance, and where had it been in the meantime?''

''Well, it's quite obvious why my father didn't approach Philip to make out the will for him,'' said Eleanor. ''It was a quite monstrous thing to do,'' she added with a quiver in her voice, ''and I'm quite sure he must have been ashamed of it. But where he put it for safekeeping, and how it came into Geraldine's possession, are a puzzle, I admit, but nothing to do with her death.''

"I think that must be a matter of opinion," said Richard tentatively.

"And if you don't think that's mysterious enough, mother," Phil put in, "what the dickens was she doing masquerading under the name of Peabody in a one-bedroom flat, even if it was a good address?"

"That, I think, is nobody's business but her own," said his mother crushingly.

"Not anymore," said Phil, shaking his head. "Her death—her murder, I should say—throws the whole thing wide open. In fairness to Malcolm—"

"I gather you share my own doubts about him, Phil," Richard said.

"Yes, I do. The questions I asked are relevant, mother, though I'm pretty sure we all know the answer. So we're left with the problem of who this Hector Peabody was."

"The police asked me that," said Eleanor thoughtfully. "But they didn't seem very concerned that I didn't know the answer. And if you're insinuating, Phil, that your Aunt Geraldine was having an affaire with this man—"

"Well, it's obvious, isn't it? There's no reason why she and Uncle Max should have rented a flat in town just to spend a few afternoons a week there alone, which is what seems to have happened. I say, Richard, you're not thinking it might have been dad, are you?"

"Philip!" said his mother awfully. "That remark is going too far, even for you."

"No, but I can see it from Richard's point of view. Dad's a will merchant; Jock might well have had second thoughts and taken the document to him for vetting."

"That would explain how it got into the apartment, certainly," said Richard noncommittally.

"All the same, I'm looking for ideas, having none of my own just yet."

"The will being there does make it look as if some member of the family might be concerned," said Phil, apparently oblivious of his mother's rising anger. "Only, you know, I can't really believe it. I can't believe it of any of my other relatives, either," he added, rather despondently.

Richard turned back to his hostess. He wasn't quite sure whether the younger man's intervention had been for good or ill. "You'll think the question impertinent, Mrs. Lawson," he said apologetically, "but were you under the impression that your sister was happily married?"

"Certainly I was." And suddenly it was as though an ice floe had broken and the words came tumbling out. "I can never forgive her for the deception," Eleanor said. "She had always such a holier-than-thou attitude, so goody-goody. If you had heard her talk when the Allinsons got divorced! And to think that all the time—"

"You see, mother, it's material who Peabody is," Phil pointed out.

"Well, I have no more idea than you have. Certainly not your father. And if you insist on it being one of the family, Mr. Trenton, that only leaves Wilf Bennett. He's a tiresome sort of man, but Alexandra dotes on him. I can't see why he'd need to look elsewhere for amusement."

"Aunt Alex and Aunt Geraldine were very different sorts of people," said Phil. "And if you want to know what I think, mother, I *don't* think Aunt Alex dotes on Wilf at all. I think she's scared of him."

"Nonsense. She has a very loving nature. A very weak one, too, I'm sorry to say," said Eleanor firmly.

And that, though Richard stayed so long that he

certainly outstayed his welcome, was all that was to
be got from her. Phil followed him out of the room
as he went, but instead of going to the front door
crossed the hall. "Come in here," he invited, and
led the way into what was obviously used as a
study. "I could see all sorts of other questions
hovering on the tip of your tongue," he said, when
they were both seated, "but you were too tactful to
ask mother. You don't need to be tactful with me."

"What is your attitude toward all this, Phil?"

"The devil's in it now, Joanna's sorry for Malcolm," said Phil ruefully. "However, that's beside
the point. I think I could see him being very angry
indeed if he'd discovered someone had been trying
to cheat him deliberately, but even so I can't see
him taking that further step. And, as you said, there
are too many questions left."

"Do you agree with me, too, that the will must
come into it somehow?"

"I think I do." He sounded a little doubtful, but
then went on more firmly. "I can quite see anyway
that you've got to take that as a starting place. If
somebody is involved outside the family, you
haven't the facilities for tracing Peabody."

"That's true. It's a starting point, that's all," said
Richard rather hurriedly.

"And what you'd like to ask my mother and
didn't dare—and don't think I blame you for that—
was for alibis for all of us for Sunday night."

"Not only Sunday night. We don't have any dates
for your Aunt Geraldine's visits to the Mayfair flat,
but it would help to know whether Mr. Bennett or
Mr. Fielding was free to join her there in the middle
of a working afternoon."

"You're being tactful again," said Phil. "You'd
like to add dad to that list, wouldn't you?"

"Since you ask me, yes."

"Well, good heavens, man, they're all in business

for themselves. I know I've often phoned dad in the afternoon and found he was out meeting a client. As for the kind of business the uncles do, that makes it even more likely for them to be absent without explanation.''

"Yes, I see. I'm not really considering your father, Phil, if only for the reason that he would be the one member of the family besides yourself who would have been very willing to include Malcolm in a settlement. There was no reason for him to suppress the will.'' But he was thinking, as he spoke, except perhaps to oblige his wife. Or, of course, there's the possibility that he was deliberately trying to deceive me.

"All right, I see that,'' said Phil. "But I can't understand why you include Uncle Max.''

"Just to be thorough,'' said Richard vaguely. "What about Sunday evening, if you don't mind telling me?''

"I don't mind, but if you remember, I was with Joanna that evening, at your place, so all I know is what I've heard in family discussions since. There was a sort of council of war on Monday after we heard the news.''

"I'm not a lawyer,'' Richard pointed out. "I'm not particularly concerned about whether evidence is hearsay or not, at this stage anyway.''

"No, I suppose you aren't. Dad was out, too. He brought some work home from the office and was in here all day dealing with it. So naturally he was restless, and went on the heath to walk it off.''

"That's natural enough.''

"Uncle Max says he was at home, and he says Aunt Geraldine told him she was going to visit Aunt Alex.''

"She never said anything to him about the will?''

"No, but you wouldn't expect her to have done so

under the circumstances, would you? I mean, if she was concealing it deliberately.''

"That's true. It just leaves the Bennetts, then.''

"Uncle Wilf was out, too. He'd gone up to town to meet a client. . . Uncle Max knew all about it. If a contract had ensued he'd most likely have been the architect. I don't suppose you want to hear about Aunt Alex, but just to round matters off she was at home. Well, she must have been, because of Virginia. That's my cousin. She's only seven, far too young to be left alone.''

"Thank you, Phil, that's very comprehensive. And very discouraging,'' he added, smiling, "but I don't suppose that displeases you too much.''

"No, it doesn't. Like you, I'd like to do something for Malcolm, but not at the expense of one of my own relations, of course. Though, I suppose,'' he added thoughtfully, "the fact that Jock included him in his will really makes it pretty certain that Malcolm was a relation, too.''

"I think it does, but then I thought that anyway. I suppose you can't think of any explanation for the will turning up like that?''

"No, I can't.''

"Or for your Aunt Geraldine asking Malcolm to go to the Mayfair flat to see her.''

"Not unless she came across the will by accident, saw the unfairness of her previous attitude, and wanted to make amends. But you say she stopped short of that.''

"That's Malcolm's story, certainly.''

"I wonder if he's telling the truth about that.''

"Jake Fulford thinks he is, and he knows him considerably better than I do. But not better than you do, I daresay. You've more in common with him than either of us, being nearer in age.''

"Yes, that's true, though sometimes I feel a hundred years older.'' He saw that Richard was getting to his feet and followed his example. "You have my blessing anyway, Richard, if you can do anything for him; then Joanna can stop being sympathetic and the matter can be decided on its merits."

"The question of which of you she prefers?" Richard asked him.

"Yes, that's right. At least now I shan't still feel I have an unfair advantage over him. Not if he's free, that is."

"I'll do my best." But Richard was thinking sadly as he followed Philip's directions and walked toward the Fieldings' house—stopping on the way for one of those curious "light lunches" that always put him in mind of Mr. P.G. Wodehouse in one of his less serious moods—that he was only tilting at windmills, and might expect to have as much success as the originator of that unlikely pastime.

III

MAXWELL FIELDING was at home. He opened the door himself to Richard and, oddly enough, seemed pleased to see him. "People have been very kind," he said, leading the way into the drawing room. This house was more modern than the Lawsons', and furnished in a modern though obviously expensive way. "It's good of you to make a special journey to express your condolences."

This, as can be imagined, momentarily took the wind out of Richard's sails. He said what he felt was proper, rather glad to be addressing Fielding's back as he did so, and apologized quite sincerely for troubling him at such a time.

"No trouble at all, I'm glad of the distraction," said Fielding. "My brother-in-law is with me—if you can call my wife's sister's husband my brother-in-law—but we know each other so well we've said all there is to say already." At the same moment

Richard saw over his shoulder the stout form of Wilfred Bennett getting up from a chair near the window.

"You again," he said, in not too friendly a tone.

"Mr. Trenton has very kindly called to tell me how sorry he is about poor Geraldine," said Fielding.

"Nonsense," said Bennett, and made a curious snorting sound that Richard interpreted as expressing disbelief. "He's a friend of Malcolm's, he told us that himself on Sunday. That's why he's here."

"Is that so?" asked Fielding. "You know I don't really want to hear any more about that wretched young man."

"Mr. Bennett is right in a way," said Richard. "Could we say I had a dual purpose in coming? I'm really sorry—"

"Yes, yes, so you told me. You'd better sit down, Mr. Trenton," said Fielding, "and tell us the real purpose of this visit." His manner was still quite gentle, a vivid contrast to Wilfred Bennett, who was quivering with anger.

"It isn't easy to explain."

"I'll bet it isn't!"

"You see," said Richard, ignoring Bennett's intervention and concentrating his attention on Maxwell Fielding, "Malcolm denies absolutely that he killed your wife. If I didn't believe him I wouldn't have dreamed of coming here, but I was hoping to find some explanation of certain things that the police theory leaves unanswered."

"I don't want to be unfair to anybody," said Fielding. "Particularly at a time like this."

"What do you mean, at a time like this?" asked Wilfred Bennett belligerently.

"I mean that, in fairness to Geraldine's memory, I shouldn't like the wrong person to be punished for her death," said Fielding.

"There's no question of that. Malcolm has been up to no good from the beginning. First he got round old Jock, then he persuaded him to make a will in his favor—"

"Only partly in his favor," Maxwell corrected him gently. "If there's any doubt in Mr. Trenton's mind that he's the guilty party, I think we should go along with him in probing it."

"All right, then, let him ask his questions and see where that gets us," said Bennett. He turned to Richard directly. "What do you want to know?" he demanded.

"There's first the question of Hector Peabody's identity," said Richard. In view of Fielding's friendliness he felt worse than ever in asking such a question, but it had to be done.

"I utterly decline to believe there is any such person," said Fielding with more firmness than he had previously shown.

"Oh, come, now, Max," Wilfred protested. "You know perfectly well Geraldine was playing fast and loose with you, there's no good trying to hide the fact."

"And you know perfectly well, Wilf, that we had an ideal relationship," said Fielding with dignity. "I believe Malcolm's story to this extent, that Gerry told him she was borrowing a friend's flat. That's obviously what happened."

"I'm afraid not," said Richard. "As I understand it she was identified as the woman who called herself Mavis Peabody by two of the tenants."

"They were mistaken, that's all. People look different when they're dead," said Fielding stubbornly.

"Well, if you're right," said Richard obligingly, leaving the question of the handwriting to one side, "perhaps you can tell me who the Peabodys are. Surely some of your friends."

"I know nobody of that name."

"Don't be an ostrich, old fellow," said Wilfred, apparently trying to be more encouraging now. "I don't agree with him, you know," he added to Richard, "but neither do I know anybody who could possibly be Hector Peabody."

"You do see that this little mystery is a point in Malcolm's favor?"

"I don't agree with you there," said Bennett. "I can see that his lawyers will probably make a great play with it in court, and I'm sorry for that, Max, it will be horribly embarrassing for you. But as for the rest—"

Richard turned to Fielding. "You know where the will was found?"

"Yes, I've been told that."

"Who do you think put it there?"

"Why, Gerry, I suppose."

"Don't you think that creates a strong presumption that she was one of the tenants of the flat? She wouldn't have hidden it where she couldn't recover it."

"No, I can't agree with you there," said Bennett. "Obviously she hid it before she sent for Malcolm, in case he should try to find it. But she wouldn't be expecting him to kill her; she could have taken it back afterward and left in the normal way."

"Then you agree with Mr. Fielding?"

"Only in part. I still think—I'm sorry, Max—there was some funny business going on. But if she got hold of the will somehow, and wanted to talk to Malcolm about it, she might well have thought that the Mayfair address was convenient for their meeting."

"I see. Where do you think she got the will from, then?"

"I can't think, unless Jock entrusted it to her."

"He'd never have done that," said Fielding, rousing himself from his apathy. "If he'd told anybody about it it would have been Alexandra. She was by far his favorite, and much more sympathetic toward Malcolm than any of us, except perhaps Philip."

"Oh, I think you're wrong there," said Wilfred Bennett easily. "Alex has far too much sense to throw money away. And you know, Max, there wasn't all that much sympathy between her and Gerry."

"No, that's perfectly true." The thought seemed to depress Maxwell Fielding.

"The question remains, why did Mrs. Fielding ask Malcolm to meet her?" said Richard.

"It doesn't solve the puzzle of how she got hold of the will, but having done so, I think, it was your talk on Sunday afternoon that must have persuaded her," said Fielding. "She'd been basing her objections to helping Malcolm on the fact that he had no right to anything of Jock's, but if she decided after all that he was her half brother, even if illegitimate, that may have made a difference."

"But she didn't tell him about the will, only asked him some questions to confirm what I'd said," Richard objected, not too pleased by this echo of Chief Inspector Denby's opinion.

"So he says," said Wilfred Bennett. "I don't think you can rely on that for a moment."

"I can't agree with you about that," said Richard, getting up, "but I'm grateful to you anyway for giving me so much of your time. Do you think, Mr. Bennett, that Mrs. Bennett would mind if I called on her in a little while?"

"Alex? There's nothing she could possibly tell you."

"It would round matters off," said Richard, assuming a dejected air, which for the moment he did not feel. "I told you I was interested in Malcolm's welfare, and that's perfectly true, but I'm also act-

ing under instructions from my superiors at the
bank, and they expect a complete report.''

"No reason why he shouldn't talk to Alex," said
Maxwell Fielding, with more energy than he had
previously shown. "Do her good to have a bit of a
break, and you told me yourself you wouldn't be
home very early tonight.''

"Oh, very well, very well. I see there's no help for
it," said Bennett. "She may have taken Virginia for
a walk after lunch," he added, glancing at his watch,
"but she'll certainly be in around four o'clock. A
great one for a cup of tea is Alex.''

So Richard renewed his thanks and made his farewells and went away leaving an uncomfortable
silence behind him. He wondered whether by any
chance either of them had any idea of what was
really in his mind.

13

It was still not much past three o'clock, so Richard didn't take the most direct route to the Bennetts' house, and being lucky enough to pass a row of shops that included a café he turned in there for a cup of tea. It would have been better to talk it over with Maggie, but there wasn't time for that. He thought he saw now the answer to his problem; proving his theory was another matter. Perhaps Jake Fulford might have better fortune, but one thing was certain...the man who called himself Hector Peabody wouldn't be going near the Mayfair flat again. Short of getting an admission there didn't seem to be much chance of identifying him and there was no earthly reason why he should admit his association with Geraldine Fielding, either.

And first there was the point to consider, why Geraldine had summoned Malcolm to see her? He didn't like the idea, but he was pretty sure now that it had been because of some doubts his own remarks to the assembled family on the Sunday afternoon had raised. He hadn't thought Geraldine a particularly sympathetic character, but perhaps there was a sense of justice buried in her somewhere; she may have felt it only right to try to satisfy herself about Malcolm's parentage. But to suggest that at the trial without further evidence would be to suggest also that she had gone still further in her talk with him, to add a point, in fact, to the police's theory of what had happened. As for

his own part in the matter, Denby's words had made
him very uncomfortable at first, but now that he had
thought it over he realized that nobody was com-
pelled to commit murder. If one was to spend one's
life worrying about the effect of one's actions, one
would probably have no peace ever again.

So he went back to his problem and turned it over
and over in his mind, stirring his tea absentmind-
edly—and unnecessarily—but not remembering to
drink it until it was almost cold. As he set down his
cup a shadow fell across the table and a well-known
voice said, with mock geniality, "So we meet again,
Mr. Trenton."

Richard looked up without speaking for a moment, seeing, as he had expected, Chief Inspector
Denby and Detective Sergeant Axtell standing beside him. "I've been thinking over what you said,
Chief Inspector," he said then without further pre-
amble. "And I've decided that the strictest judge
couldn't hold me responsible for what happened to
Mrs. Fielding."

"Not legally, of course," said Denby, taking the
remark quite seriously. "But morally . . . yes, I think
so."

"Then we must agree to differ. Why don't you
and the sergeant sit down? I was just going to ask
for another pot of tea."

"What are you doing in this part of the world?"
asked Denby, obeying this injunction. "I suppose
you've been harassing the members of Jock Thorold's family again."

"I've been talking to them," said Richard. "Some
of them were friendly and some of them were unfriendly, but none of them seemed particularly
harassed. And I don't see why they should be, do
you?"

"*I* don't," said Denby emphasizing the words,
"but I rather thought you did."

"Well, as to that, we shall see." He raised his hand and signaled to the waitress. "I'd like some more tea if you don't mind," he said, "and I think these gentlemen will join me."

"You seem rather pleased with yourself," said Axtell. As usual when he broke his silence, it came as a surprise to the others. "Do I take it your inquiries have reached some conclusion?"

"No, Sergeant, not yet. I'm putting in a little time here until four o'clock when I'm assured Mrs. Bennett will be at home. After that there will be nothing else I can do."

"Except perhaps talk to Mr. Fulford," said Axtell shrewdly. "Unless of course your inquiries have tended to confirm the case against his client."

"That would be between Mr. Fulford and myself," Richard pointed out.

"It obviously isn't that, Sergeant," said Denby rather angrily. "You pointed out yourself that Mr. Trenton is looking smug, and as he has dedicated himself to proving Malcolm Stonor's innocence I imagine he thinks he's on to something."

"As I said, Chief Inspector, that would be a matter for the defense."

The tea arrived at that moment and they were silent while it was being served. "What would you say," said Denby when the waitress had gone away again, "if I told you that we were on our way to Mrs. Bennett's, too?"

"Do you want to see her or her husband?"

"Either, or both."

"Well, you won't see him. He was with Mr. Fielding earlier and I understand he expected to go back to his office and would be rather late home. But if you want to see Mrs. Bennett I'll wait until you've finished."

"That's kind of you, I'm sure. However, I've a

better suggestion, Mr. Trenton. Why don't we go all together?"

Richard frowned over that. "What are you getting at, Chief Inspector?" he asked.

"Have you any objection?"

That was an awkward one. Truth to tell he had every objection but he didn't feel it politic to say so. "I don't mind at all," said Richard airily, "but I'd thought it would have been difficult for you, making an official inquiry in the presence of an outsider."

"I hardly think of you as an outsider anymore," said Denby sarcastically. "We seem to have fallen into each other's paths so often lately I almost think of you as one of the family."

"I must say, I appreciate that," said Richard, and exchanged a smile with Axtell. "All the same, I think—"

"You don't want to share this idea—whatever it is—with us," said Denby accusingly.

"Nothing like that."

"Then you think I might object to your questions."

"If you knew how few of them there are," said Richard, and smiled again. "But I'm wondering, Chief Inspector, why do *you* want to see the lady?"

"Routine, that's all. When we saw the rest of the family on Monday it happened that we didn't see her. She was out with the little girl on the heath, and as it didn't seem important we didn't press the matter. But, of course, the inquiry has to be rounded off."

"Of course," Richard echoed. And all of a sudden he made up his mind. "All right, we'll go together," he said, "and the devil take the hindmost. But first I'm going to drink my tea."

II

THE WALK round to the Bennetts' house, after the tea had been drunk to the last drop, left Richard feeling very much as though he was under arrest. Denby and Axtell walked one on each side of him and didn't liven the journey with much conversation. Once Denby said, "Still feeling so self-confident, Mr. Trenton?" in a mocking tone, and Richard replied, "That was only Sergeant Axtell's idea." Otherwise they went their way in silence.

Alexandra Bennett let them in, and her eyes widened in something like panic when she saw the three men on the doorstep. Then she focused on Richard and seemed to recognize him. "Mr. Trenton," she said, "what are you doing here again? And who are these men?"

Richard told her. "I gather their wanting to talk to you is merely a matter of routine, Mrs. Bennett, because they missed you the other day. And it wasn't my idea that we should come here together, but Chief Inspector Denby doesn't altogether trust my motives. And my methods still less," he added smiling.

"I don't quite know what you mean," she said backing away, "but if it's the police, of course they must come in." She turned to the fair-haired little girl who was standing a few feet behind her. "Virginia, go and play very quietly in your own room. Mummy will be downstairs if you want her."

The child turned obediently, after a last curious look at the three invaders. "That's all right, then, come in here," said Alexandra nervously, and led the way into her drawing room. This resembled neither of her sisters', being comfortable in a rather shabby way. "Father was always telling me I should redecorate," said Alexandra nervously, obviously aware that her domain was under scrutiny. "In fact he even offered to pay for it himself once, but I like things just as they are. Besides, after Virginia came along—we'd been married quite a number of years then—I thought everything should be left as it was until she was a little bit more grown."

"I think it's a very nice room, Mrs. Bennett," said Richard with some truth. "Don't you, Sergeant?" he queried Axtell, as being probably the more sympathetic of the two detectives. Axtell murmured something in agreement, and then the chief inspector took charge of the proceedings.

"Perhaps, Mrs. Bennett, you will be good enough to sit down, then we can all make ourselves comfortable," he suggested. "As Mr. Trenton told you when he introduced us there are one or two questions, but they are purely routine, particularly in the circumstances that have since arisen."

"He means Malcolm Stonor's arrest," said Richard. He sustained a furious look from the detective with equanimity and went to seat himself at the farthest end of the room, markedly dissociating himself from the police inquiries.

"Oh, poor Malcolm," said Alexandra, clasping her hands together. "It's terribly hard to believe."

"You don't have to believe it," said Richard, looking out of the window.

"Oh, but Wilfred says it's quite obvious what happened. There can't be any doubt of it surely?" she said, looking at Denby for confirmation.

"That's not for me to say, Mrs. Bennett," Denby said heavily. "He's been committed for trial, you know, and now it's up to the jury. Mr. Trenton has his own view of things, which is not the official one, but you don't have to take any notice of him."

"I'm sure he means well," said Alexandra, rather reprovingly. "Do you have some questions for me, Chief Inspector? What are they?"

"Had your sister Geraldine ever mentioned to you the flat in Mayfair?"

"No, of course she hadn't." This was said very definitely, with no doubt in her tone at all. "It was obviously a thing she wouldn't mention to anyone," she added, "and I'm surprised you should ask me that."

"I said it was routine, Mrs. Bennett, but there are certain things I'm afraid I must ask you. Did she tell you anything about your father's will? That she knew he'd made one, for instance?"

"She didn't tell me anything like that."

"And so you have no idea how she came by it?"

This time she looked down at her hands. "I believe I have already answered that question, Chief Inspector," she said, gently rebuking.

"She didn't tell you where she was going that evening?"

She looked him full in the face then. "No, she didn't," she said, with some indignation. "In fact I believe she told Max she was coming to see me, which I don't think was at all fair."

"Did you know she intended to ask Malcolm Stonor to meet her?"

"I'm sure you've already realized that I was not in my sister's confidence, Chief Inspector."

"You yourself were at home all evening, and she didn't even call for a few moments to give a semblance of truth to her story?"

"No, Chief Inspector, she did not."

"Very well, Mrs. Bennett, we'll leave it there. But there's another question I must ask you and I'm afraid it's also one you won't like. You know that the flat in Mayfair was rented in the names of Mr. and Mrs. Hector Peabody. Have you any idea who Hector Peabody could have been?"

This time the answer was so long in coming that Richard turned from the window and looked at her

wonderingly. "I know nobody of that name," Alexandra said at last.

"Could it have been any of your friends?"

"Chief Inspector, I'm sure you must realize this is
very difficult for me, very embarrassing. No, I can't
think it possible that Geraldine was having an affaire with any of our friends."

"Oh, well, I think in the circumstances we may
disregard Mr. Peabody," said Denby almost genial-
ly. "Though I'm sure Mr. Trenton here won't agree
with me. Will you, Mr. Trenton?"

"I don't agree with you at all," said Richard. "I
think Mr. Peabody is the very essence of the case."
His eyes were fixed on Alexandra Bennett as he
spoke. She was still flushed, but calmer than she
had been. "Are you handing me the floor now,
Chief Inspector?" he inquired.

"If you can think of any further questions for
Mrs. Bennett," said Denby. "I think myself I've
covered everything."

"Do you, indeed?"

"She is on the very periphery of the case, Mr.
Trenton. What other conceivable questions could
you have to ask her? She's already told us everything she knows."

"Then I daresay you'd like to leave us," Richard
suggested.

"I will leave when you do. That is, with Mrs. Bennett's permission," said Denby politely. "I ask you
again, Mr. Trenton, what else could you possibly
have to ask this lady, when she has already answered me very fully?"

"You are occupied with your questions, Chief
Inspector. I wonder if you bother to listen to the answers. In the circumstances, as you yourself would
say . . . meaning that Malcolm Stonor has been arrested and you believe him guilty."

"I hope I know my duty, Mr. Trenton," said Denby stiffly.

"Oh, I'm sure you do. I'm only suggesting you're suffering at the moment from an *idée fixe*. You've made up your mind—"

"If we're to talk about making up one's mind," said Denby, speaking rather angrily, "I don't think you should leave yourself out of the discussion, Mr. Trenton."

"No, I, too, am working from a certain premise. But I did listen to Mrs. Bennett's answers to your questions—Sergeant Axtell has them written down and will confirm what I say. Most of them were evasive; where she couldn't avoid answering altogether she told you the literal truth, and sometimes, I believe, with the intention of conveying exactly the opposite meaning. Or she took refuge in indignation. Am I right, Sergeant?"

Axtell looked up from his notebook, frowning. "I've no means of knowing, Mr. Trenton," he said a trifle apologetically. "There were one or two occasions when I admit it seemed that Mrs. Bennett was being evasive, not answering quite directly. And she was certainly indignant that her sister had told Mr. Fielding that she was going to visit her the evening she was murdered. As for being literal—"

"Refer to the chief inspector's question about where Mrs. Fielding had acquired the will." He paused a moment while Axtell ruffled through the pages of his notebook. "Have you got it?"

The sergeant nodded. "Mrs. Bennett said, 'She didn't tell me anything like that.'"

"And how are we to know that isn't the exact truth?" said Denby aggressively.

"I have a few questions to ask Mrs. Bennett, with her permission of course, but with or without yours, Chief Inspector." Richard turned to Alexandra. "The other members of your family, Mrs. Bennett, have been kind enough to talk to me. I hope you'll be willing to help me, too."

"Very willing, Mr. Trenton, if I could see in what way I could be of help to you." Her eyes were on Sergeant Axtell's notebook as she spoke.

"I've no right to ask you questions," Richard told her, "and no notes will be made of your answers. But I should like to ask them in the presence of the chief inspector and the sergeant, again if you'll permit me."

"You've been talking to Eleanor," she said, rather hesitantly.

"Yes, I have. I spoke to her earlier today. And to her husband, and to your husband, too; he was with Mr. Fielding at the time."

"I see." The resolution with which she had answered his first question seemed to be fading now, but she managed something very like a titter of amusement. "It would be very odd in me if I refused to talk to you as they have done, wouldn't it?" she said.

"Mr. Trenton has absolutely no right—" Denby began, but she silenced him with a gesture.

"I've said I'll try to help him, Chief Inspector."

"Thank you, Mrs. Bennett." Now that the point was reached, all Richard's self-confidence seemed to have drained out of him. "First of all I want to go back to the time when your father was still alive."

"You're thinking that Malcolm was resentful because he wasn't remembered in my father's will. And then he found he had been after all—"

"Nothing like that, Mrs. Bennett. Could we take this my way? Perhaps after all we should go back four or five years, to the time when Malcolm Stonor first came to live with your father. He never explained his reasons for taking the boy to live with him. . . or did he?" Alexandra made no answer to that and after a while he went on. "Your sisters, Eleanor and Geraldine, were very much against this move, and still more when the question of possible adoption came up. I think it was because of their opposition that the matter was dropped, and also for that reason that Mr. Thorold decided against making a will."

"But he did make a will," said Alexandra. "It was found when Geraldine died."

"Yes, we know all about that. Your husband, too, was very much against anything being done for Malcolm. That's right, isn't it?"

"He agreed with Eleanor and Geraldine."

"And you agreed with him?"

"Of course I did."

"I wonder if that's true. I have a suggestion to make to you, Mrs. Bennett, that although in public you followed your husband's lead, in private you were uneasy about the stand the family was taking against Malcolm Stonor. Was it because you believed he might in fact be Jock Thorold's illegitimate son?"

"No...no! I just thought that he was a boy from the slums, who'd been catapulted into quite a different way of life. It can't have been easy for him, but then it would have been very unfair to leave him in midair, as it were, to go back where he came from."

All at once Richard was conscious of Denby's heavy breathing and prayed briefly that the chief inspector would not intervene just then. Sergeant Axtell was fiddling with his pen, probably itching to put it to work. "That was why you went to your father and persuaded him to make a will on the lines he had originally intended, wasn't it?" asked Richard, and paused, allowing the silence to lengthen. "You were his favorite daughter, weren't you, Mrs. Bennett?"

"Yes, I . . . I think he had a specially soft place in his heart for me because I was the youngest," said Alexandra.

"You don't like lying, do you, Mrs. Bennett?"

"No, I . . . well, perhaps it was at my suggestion. It seemed only fair. And the reason I did it was the one I gave you, but then my father admitted to me that Malcolm was his son."

"So you knew all about the will. What happened then, Mrs. Bennett?"

"Nothing . . . nothing!"

"Tell me at least what was said between you about it."

"My father only said he knew perfectly well how to make a—a holograph will, isn't it called? So he didn't have to consult Philip or anyone else about it, and of course I could rely on his knowing what he was doing."

"And what happened then?"

"He said since I was the one with Malcolm's interests at heart he'd give it into my keeping. But he said, because the others objected so strongly, I wasn't to tell anyone about it."

"When was this, Mrs. Bennett?"

"Oh, not long ago, two or three weeks before he fell."

"And did you obey his instructions?"

"Of course I did!"

"How, then, did the will come into your sister Geraldine Fielding's possession?"

"I don't know. I really don't know, Mr. Trenton."

"But still you allowed it to be assumed that Mr. Thorold had died intestate. I think you're going to have to explain that—to the chief inspector if not to me."

"Mr. Trenton certainly seems to have a valid point there, Mrs. Bennett," said Denby unwillingly.

"I don't know, I don't know. They were all so set against me."

Richard said quickly before the detective could speak, "Your husband, Wilfred Bennett, is a very forceful man, isn't he? How long have you known about the liaison between him and your sister, Geraldine Fielding?"

"Mr. Trenton, this is intolerable," said Denby. "I've been very patient, but—"

"Your patience doesn't come into it, Chief Inspector. It's only Mrs. Bennett's indulgence that I need."

Alexandra was staring at him now rather as though she was mesmerized. "How did you know?" she whispered.

"I'm a banker, Mrs. Bennett, so let's say I put two and two together. You confirmed my surmise when the chief inspector asked you about Hector Peabody, and you replied very precisely, 'I know nobody of that name.' I mentioned before that on a number of occasions your answers were very evasive, and that was a particularly glaring instance."

"I didn't blame Wilfred. I. . . Geraldine was a so much more forceful personality," she said apologetically.

"No." Richard spoke gently now. "I think you love your husband very much, don't you?"

"Oh, I do, I do!"

"And it didn't take him very long to get the truth out of you about the will?"

"I realized I had no right to keep a thing like that from him."

"What was his reaction?"

She was looking down at her hands, clasping and unclasping in her lap. "I think he was very angry, but he didn't say anything then. Only that it was a wicked thing I had done, unjust to the rest of the family, even to our own Virginia. I think that was the trouble, really. She's the sun and the moon and the stars to him, after we had to wait so long for her. And then he said he would keep the will himself, because it would be safer with him than with me.''

''I can see he wouldn't destroy it with your father still alive, but I wonder why he didn't afterward.''

''I think that's obvious,'' she said sadly. ''My father might have told somebody. He told Mr. Blake at the bank of his intentions, you know that. He might have told him that the will had been actually made.''

''Yes, that makes sense,'' said Richard slowly. ''What did Mr. Bennett do with the will?''

''I don't know.''

''Was it put away in your house?''

''Oh, I'm quite sure it wasn't. To tell you the truth, Mr. Trenton, I looked everywhere after father died. But even before I did I was quite sure it wasn't here, I know every nook and cranny of this place.''

''At his office, then?''

She smiled a little sadly. ''I don't think that, either. His secretary is a good girl, but she's into everything. He would never have felt it was safe there.''

''Just a minute, Mr. Trenton.'' Denby had come to his feet. ''You do realize the conclusion we must draw from this, Mrs. Bennett? That your husband took Mr. Thorold's will to the flat in Mayfair that he shared with your sister under the name of Peabody, and that she found it there.''

''He told her,'' said Alexandra simply.

''How do you know that?''

Sergeant Axtell was writing again. She watched him in silence for a moment, and then said sadly, ''I know. Couldn't we leave it at that?''

''I'm afraid, Mrs. Bennett, we can't leave it

there." He paused, and it was quite obvious that the picture a defense counsel might draw of three large men intimidating one weak woman was very clear in his mind. "Would you like to talk to a solicitor, yours or your husband's, before we go any further?"

"No, no, there's no need. I just think I won't say any more."

"Mrs. Bennett," Richard ventured to intervene. "Would you like Chief Inspector Denby to spell out to you the implications of what you've told us?"

"It was you who said that I didn't like lying, Mr. Trenton. I've admitted Wilfred was having an affaire with another woman, with my own sister. Isn't that enough for you?"

"Have you forgotten that Malcolm Stonor has been arrested?"

She closed her eyes for a moment, as though that might blot out the truth of what he was saying. "You said what I told you had certain implications, Chief Inspector," she said then. "Perhaps I should hear them."

"I think you should." Denby's tone was a little grim now, but the look he shot at Richard was no more friendly than before. "You say you know that Mr. Bennett told Mrs. Fielding the will existed, and I think you'll agree there is a very strong supposition that he kept it at the Mayfair flat. Mrs. Fielding, as we know, was very much against anything being done in Stonor's favor, but it may be that she changed or considered changing her opinion after Mr. Trenton's intervention last Sunday. She talked to Stonor the night she died. Suppose it is as he said, that he left her alive. Might she not then have told her lover that she had changed her mind, that in fairness the will should be produced—"

"No, no! It wasn't like that at all. Wilfred wasn't there that evening, nor anywhere near the flat."

To Richard's dismay there was a ring of truth in

her voice. He got to his feet and ranged himself beside the chief inspector. "How do you know that,
Mrs. Bennett?" he asked gently, and as he spoke il-
lumination hit him. Of all the fools. . . !

"Because he hadn't the keys. He left them on the
top of the tallboy," she said, almost as though she
were proud of his carelessness. "He always used to
do things like that, he never could keep a secret
from me."

Beside him Richard could feel that Denby's anger
was rising, almost as though there was some physical manifestation of this. "And what did you do
with the keys, Mrs. Bennett?" he asked quickly.

"You can't say Wilfred did it," she said again.

"I'm not saying anything of the kind, but unless
you tell us—"

"I gave them to Eleanor, of course. You'd guessed
that, hadn't you?"

"Perhaps I had," Richard agreed. "But in fairness
to your husband I think you should tell the chief inspector—"

"I'll tell him anything, anything. I can't let him
think. . .such dreadful things."

"Well, then?" said Richard. Denby silenced him
with a glance.

"If you want to make a statement, Mrs. Bennett—" he suggested.

"Yes, of course I do. Mr. Trenton was quite right,
I don't like telling lies. And it isn't fair to Malcolm,
I've known that all along. But Wilfred wouldn't
have done anything to harm Gerry."

"We'll sit down again," said Denby, putting the
action to the words, "and Sergeant Axtell will write
down what you have to tell us. You say that your
sister, Mrs. Eleanor Lawson, had the keys of the
Mayfair flat. How long had she had them?"

"She came here that evening. Quite early as a
matter of fact. She said Geraldine had told her ev-

erything, about the will and about the place in Mayfair where she was to meet Malcolm. And, of
course, I wasn't the only one who knew about Wilf
and Gerry; Eleanor hadn't been told but she knew
quite well, too. So she guessed that was the meeting
place and said that producing the will was something that just couldn't be allowed to happen. Well,
Eleanor could always make me do just what she
wanted. I gave her the keys.''

"Do you know what happened after that?'' said
Richard, earning another dirty look from the chief
inspector.

"Only that she returned them much later in the
evening. I thought she seemed a little upset, but
with Eleanor it's always difficult to tell.''

III

"I SUPPOSE YOU REALIZE,'' said Denby grumpily five
minutes later, "that Mrs. Lawson might quite well
have been upset if she'd used the keys and had gone
in and found her sister dead?'' He'd asked permission to talk to Mr. Trenton privately in another
room, leaving the sergeant to transcribe his notes
and get Alexandra Bennett's signature.

"Of course I realize it, but I think you're going to
have to ask her about that, don't you?''

"Naturally,'' growled Denby. "You're working
on the theory now that she killed Mrs. Fielding, are
you?''

"Aren't you, Chief Inspector? I should have said,
in view of everything, that it was obvious.''

"Then how do you explain the evidence of the
neighbor who says that Malcolm Stonor was the
only visitor?''

"You're forgetting, Chief Inspector, Mrs. Lawson
had a key. She is also very like her sister; I think
that at the distance your witness might very well

have taken one for the other. I think Mrs. Fielding concealed the will after her interview, because she was afraid that Wilfred Bennett wouldn't agree with her intention to produce it.''

"You believe that was her intention, then?''

"Something of the sort must have been in her mind or she wouldn't have sent for Malcolm. As for talking to her sister Eleanor, I think the two of them were always very close. I expect she was surprised that Mrs. Lawson turned up after Malcolm left, but told her what she had decided and tried to persuade her to the same point of view. Eleanor... you know, Chief Inspector, she's a very forceful woman, as forceful in her own way as Wilfred Bennett. We've all been considering this a man's crime, but I can quite see Eleanor losing her temper sufficiently to do what was done.''

"You're forgetting one thing, Mr. Trenton. The witness we spoke of also says that nobody left the house.''

"I have an idea about that, too,'' said Richard, rather apologetically now. "I think she was asked about the time before Mr. Weatherby came home. If you remember he had to go upstairs to his own flat to telephone. If Eleanor had stayed in the bedroom, she might easily have left as soon as he did that. If your witness was of an exact turn of mind, and the question was worded a certain way, she may have answered quite literally.''

"Very well, then, Mr. Trenton, very well.'' That was Denby at his most ominous. "We shall talk to Mrs. Lawson, of course, as soon as Sergeant Axtell has finished here. And if it turns out that your theories have no substance,'' he added with some satisfaction, "I think after Mrs. Bennett has told the rest of the family what happened they may not be inclined to take a particularly indulgent view of your activities.''

IV

WHEN HE LEFT the Bennetts' house with the two detectives still in possession, Richard walked aimlessly for a very long time. It wasn't until he was thoroughly tired out that he decided it was time he was getting home, and that in the circumstances a taxi wouldn't be too extravagant. As they went he began to wonder how Maggie would have taken his prolonged absence; knowing the change of routine she wasn't likely to be too worried, but all the same she would be wondering.

Naturally Jake Fulford would have gone home long since. When he let himself into the flat there was only Maggie in the hall to greet him, and he realized for the first time that it was already well past Ricky's bedtime. "I can't tell you how sorry I am," he began, and broke off seeing his wife with a finger to her lips.

"He's asleep," she hissed. "Come into the living room." But she added, as soon as they were safely there with the door closed, "Darling, Richard, you look dreadful."

"To tell you the truth," Richard admitted, "I don't feel my best at the moment. There's nothing wrong," he added quickly, seeing the flare of anxiety in her eyes. "I mean, I'm not ill or anything. It's just that things have come to a head, and I'm not quite sure how it will turn out."

"I'll get you a drink," said Maggie, "and then you can tell me. Unless you'd like your supper first; it's getting quite late."

"A drink will be admirable. Unless you're dying of hunger yourself waiting for me."

"No, I had a feeling you might be late so I had something with Ricky." She stood so that he couldn't see what she was doing as she poured his drink, and lied bluntly, "It's mostly water," when he protested at its size. "All right," she said, "tell me."

So he went back over the events of the day, and not very happily. "I really thought Wilfred Bennett was the guilty party," he said, when he reached the talk with Alexandra. "When she said he hadn't had his keys with him that evening she was obviously telling the truth, and I was completely thrown out of my stride for a moment. And then all of a sudden I realized . . . well, I've told you how much Mrs. Bennett admitted, but Eleanor is a tough nut. Denby will certainly press her, but I don't see him getting a confession."

"What will happen, then?" asked Maggie in a worried tone. "Mrs. Bennett's statement was taken officially, I understand that, but she's bound to tell her family how it came about."

"So Denby pointed out to me."

"They couldn't sue you for—for slander, or anything like that, could they?"

Richard cast his mind back over the interview. "So far as I remember I didn't make any suggestions to her that she didn't afterward confirm," he said, "and even if they could I doubt if they would. This business of Wilfred and Geraldine being lovers is bad enough, but Jake Fulford will be interested in that now we've identified Hector Peabody definitely. And Eleanor had some reason for wanting the key to the flat; that will take a bit of explaining."

"Then I daresay they'll all go in a body and take their accounts away from the bank," said Maggie tragically. "All except Malcolm Stonor, of course." She looked at him wide-eyed for a moment, and then unexpectedly she began to laugh. "I know it isn't funny," she said when she could speak again, "but I would like to see Mr. Jarvis's face if that happened."

"To tell you the truth, Maggie, I'm just about fed

up with the general managers' demands on my time," said Richard. "I'm not in the mood, to put it bluntly, to pull my punches if Jarvis tries to start anything."

"I've always said we'd end up in a country branch, a *small* country branch," said Maggie. "Probably one of those one-man ones that are only open twice a week." She didn't sound too dismayed by the prospect.

"They don't work quite like that," said Richard, and was about to explain when he caught Maggie's eyes and saw that she was still laughing at him. "I'm much more likely to be out on my ear," he told her bluntly.

"I know, Richard, darling, but we can manage somehow. And you never know, everything may turn out for the best. Aren't you going to ring Mr. Fulford and tell him what you found out?"

"I shall have to, of course, but you know what he'll say?"

"I should think he'd be very pleased."

"The very least he'll say is that I should have run like a hare when I met Denby and Axtell, and waited until I could see Mrs. Bennett alone."

"Well, if he does I think it's very unfair of him," said Maggie, suddenly on her dignity. Before either of them could speak again they heard the telephone ringing in the other room.

Richard went to answer it with a sense of foreboding. Denby, to gloat over my wrongheadedness, he thought as he lifted the receiver, and was surprised to hear Jake Fulford's excited voice in his ear.

"You'll never believe what's happened," the solicitor told him. "They're going to release Malcolm Stonor after all!"

"How did that come about?" asked Richard, trying to conceal his own elation.

"It seems Alexandra Bennett made a statement. Her husband was Hector Peabody all the time, and Geraldine's lover. And then she thought he might get blamed for the murder, too, and she said he didn't even have the keys of the Mayfair flat that night. Her sister Eleanor had been in Geraldine's confidence about the meeting with Malcolm, and came and bullied Alexandra into handing over the keys. After that it was a question of getting Eleanor's statement. There was a bit of a row about that, I gather; she wanted to see the detectives alone and her husband demanded to be there. He got his own way finally, and when he heard the whole story, he must have found her answers unsatisfactory, because finally, under his advice, she made a full confession. Only, of course, she's saying she saw red when Geraldine told her she meant to produce the will, so I expect they'll plead diminished responsibility, don't you?"

"Something like that, I suppose. I wouldn't have thought Eleanor Lawson would be so easily broken down."

"I don't know the details. Denby promised to see me tomorrow and give me them so that I can set the wheels in motion to get Malcolm released. Only I thought you'd want to know about it straightaway."

"I did indeed," said Richard, genuinely grateful. "In fact you don't know what a weight you've taken off my mind."

"You haven't told me how you got on today."

"That will do tomorrow, too. But you can't call it a happy ending," he said a moment later, putting down the phone, to Maggie, who had been listening at his elbow. "None of the family deserves a thing like this, and as for Philip Lawson and young Phil, they're a thoroughly nice pair of chaps."

"I know," said Maggie sympathetically. She'd

been well aware from the moment he came in that there was no easy way out, and that either he would have failed in his task and Malcolm Stonor would be tried and probably convicted, or he would have succeeded, and been thoroughly unhappy over the pain he was causing other people. But, luckily perhaps, neither had time to brood on this for long. Maggie was just saying, "You'll feel better when you've had your dinner," and he had followed her out into the hall, when Ricky in his night attire burst upon them.

"You wouldn't be so late if something hadn't happened," he asserted. "Is that man you like still in prison?"

"He won't be for long, Ricky," Richard told him.

"There, you see, I knew it would be all right if you took a hand. You found out who really did it, didn't you?"

"The police did."

"Well, I bet you helped them. I knew as soon as Chief Inspector Denby came here that that's what he wanted." Maggie and Richard exchanged a rueful glance. "And I'm going back to bed straightaway," said Ricky, obviously thinking some plot was being hatched between them. "But tell me first, did you suspect the real murderer, daddy? Did you?"

Richard nodded his head. "Well, then!" said Ricky, well satisfied. "It was my telling you to look for the most unlikely person that did it. Isn't that right?"

"I think that inspired me," said Richard solemnly. But seeing his father's expression Ricky, for once in his life, made no protest when Maggie again suggested bed.

Epilogue

AFTER THAT things went back to normal, and if Richard got no congratulations on his part in the affair, at least there were no repercussions from his superiors at the bank, either. He had to sustain a certain amount of gratitude from Malcolm Stonor, but soon persuaded that young man that any expression of obligation was unnecessary. Denby, to his relief, kept his name out of things, and—also to his relief—he didn't see the chief inspector again before the trial. On the day that Eleanor Lawson was convicted, however, he was surprised to receive a telephone call in the evening from Sergeant Axtell to tell him of the verdict. "Five years!" said Richard, surprised. "So Jake Fulford was right, they did go for diminished responsibility."

"Yes, I think they'd have liked to get away with manslaughter, but the judge wasn't buying that," said Axtell. "But I had a message for you from the chief inspector, Mr. Trenton."

"What was that?" asked Richard uneasily.

The solemnity of Axtell's tone told its own story. "Merely that you would see now that these things are better left to the police," he said.

It was three months after that that Richard saw Phil Lawson again. The young man came to the flat in Eden Place one evening and said rather abruptly, "We're getting married. We'd like you to be there."

"You and Miss Martin?" said Richard cautiously.

"Joanna, yes, of course. You'll be getting a formal invitation, you and Mrs. Trenton, but I thought I'd better tell you we'd really like you to come. Otherwise you might just tear it up and throw it away.''

"We shouldn't have done that,'' Maggie protested. "Only...are you sure?''

"Quite sure.'' He turned to Richard. "You thought I might hate you, didn't you?''

"That would certainly have been a natural reaction.''

"Well, I don't. Supposing Malcolm had gone to prison, and we'd found out later...Aunt Alexandra would be sure to tell somebody, you know. It might have been me, and then what should I have done?''

"No, I see the difficulty. But tell me about this wedding of yours. You know we wish you very happy. But you were in some doubt as to whether Joanna would have you, if Malcolm were equally well placed financially.''

"Yes, that's the good thing about it,'' said Phil. Perhaps his tone lacked some of its former buoyancy, but not too much. "This way it was a fair fight. I expect you could even say that at the moment Malcolm is better placed financially than I am. But Joanna says he's only a boy, much too young to think of getting married.''

"I see,'' said Richard, and exchanged a long look with his wife, remembering the days of their own courtship.

"A fragment of a happy ending at least,'' he said to Maggie after their visitor had gone.

The Press Raves about Raven House!

"Hard-hitting, fast-paced and cleverly constructed."
—*The Seattle Daily Times*

"I predict nothing but good for this new series."
—John Stephenson in *Mystery News*

"These books...have created much interest among mystery collectors."
—*Wilson Library Bulletin*

"Gives mystery addicts a lot to cheer about."
—*Cincinnati Post*

"Spine-tingling suspense stories sure to test your sense of adventure if not downright curdle your blood."
—*Quality Magazine*